Cedar Grove Medical:

Book One

Marissa Dobson

Published by Sunshine Press
Printed in the United States of America
ISBN-13: 978-1-939978-48-6

*D*edication

To my husband who has supported me through thick and thin.

To my readers who helped me with the research necessary for this book. For sharing your stories of hope, courage, and devastation.

To everyone who pushed for this book. My wonderful editor, Rosa, my beta readers, and proofers you're an amazing team.

Hope's Toy Chest: Cedar Grove Medical

Contents

At thirty-one, Kingsley Mathews has been named the head of the pediatric oncology department at one of the best children's hospitals in the country—Ceder Grove Children's Hospital. His life is dedicated to his patients—until one Christmas when he learns there's more than his work.

Chelsea Waters lost her daughter two years ago on Christmas Day to a rare form of childhood cancer. Her career was over, then her marriage. Now all she has left is Hope's Toy Chest. The toy drive she started in the memory of her daughter has become her everything.

When she ends up flat on her back in a pile of snow, she begins to wonder if there's room in her heart for anything more. Could the doctor who worked so feverishly to save her daughter bring the meaning of Christmas back into her heart?

Hope's Toy Chest: Cedar Grove Medical

Chapter One

Another armload of toys thudded onto the last remaining spot on the floor of the guest room, obscuring the patch of blue carpet beneath. With three weeks until Christmas, Kingsley Mathews had no idea how he'd be able to fit more toys into the small space. He could barely open the door, not to mention there was absolutely nowhere to walk except over the gifts. How he'd managed to get tangled up into all of this was beyond his imagination.

"If you could just grab the last bunch in my truck, that's all of them for now!" Elizabeth's shrill hollering reminded him how he'd gotten roped into it.

That darling little sister of his had a heart of gold, and a face that was nearly impossible to say no to. So instead of having an empty guest room gathering dust, as most bachelors did, his had become the warehouse for Hope's Toy Chest. He believed in the cause. He'd picked up toys, and even spent the days before Christmas wrapping presents with Elizabeth, but the idea of storing everything at his place had become almost too much for him. There were toys everywhere, and almost constant phone calls, emails, and unannounced visitors dropping things off. His patience was wearing thin.

Being a pediatric oncologist at one of the best children's hospitals in the country, he worked long, hard hours. He saw so much suffering, children sick and death with little he could do for them. It was a hard field, but one he chose at a young age. He strove to make a difference, and he knew finding a cure would do that. His love of children had brought him into this toy drive, and he couldn't back out now.

This year Christmas seemed to mean even less to him. There was a young girl under his care that might not make it that long. The family was hanging on, praying for a miracle that he honestly didn't believe would come. It was heartbreaking to watch them sit at her bedside every day hoping for any news that might save their daughter.

Looking around the room only stressed him more, sending his thoughts back to one of the nurses.

It will be a blessing when her time comes, no more pain and suffering.

Those words rang in his ears. There had never been a time when he thought one of his patients were better off if their time came, taking them from this world, from their loved ones. That's where he and the nurse differed. He wanted to save them all. Losing even one of them was devastating, because they had so much life left. A life they didn't get to begin living. Being surrounded by machines, needles, hospital staff, sick from the medication that was supposed to make them better. None of it was fair. They were children; they deserved a chance to live.

"Earth to Le." Elizabeth ran her hand in front of his face, shattering his thoughts sharply as though she were breaking a thin pane of glass.

"Sorry." He blinked a few times, trying to clear his mind, but his thoughts wouldn't let go of that little girl.

"Don't worry, I brought in the last of the toys." She sat them on top of another pile before looking back at him. "Hey, you okay?"

"Fine." The minute the word left his mouth, he knew he had been snippy. He and Elizabeth had always been close; their past experiences had made that bond stronger. "Sorry, I just have a lot on my mind."

"Stress at work?"

"When isn't there stress at work?" He tried to make light of it, as if it didn't bother him.

"I'm sure you haven't eaten yet, let me make you something."

She was out the door and down the hall before his brain could wrap itself around what she said. "Shit." He mumbled to himself before following after her. "Honestly, I'm fine. I already ate at the hospital. I've got to get some work done." Okay, not actual work. Instead, he wanted to read over every note of that girl's file and see if there was something he missed, something that would save her life. Damn it, he didn't want to lose her, not this close to Christmas.

"Le, you work too hard, you need to take a break sometime. Are you even taking time off for the holidays?" Elizabeth stood in the foyer where he caught her with her arms crossed over her chest.

"I'm taking off Christmas so I can help you deliver the toys as you asked."

"Shall I read between the lines? What you really mean to say is you're on call on Christmas, right?" The annoyance was clear in her voice.

"What do you want me to do, Elizabeth? Leave my patients to die so I can have off a crummy holiday that has become so commercialized that people have lost the true meaning of the season?"

"It's not just about Christmas, you never take time off. It's always work with you." Elizabeth grabbed her jacket off the back of the sofa.

"I have people depending on me. That's more important than time off to sit around and do nothing anyway." He was angry that Elizabeth of all people didn't understand. All those years ago when he decided what he was going to do with his life, years of school, and dedication, she stood by him. Now that he was finally making a name for himself, taking over the lead pediatric oncologist at only thirty-one, he couldn't let anything slide.

"Hospitals consumed our lives for years, and now they still do for you. Why can't you see that's unhealthy? You need a life outside of the hospital. When you're not there, you're here sleeping. You have no social life and a romantic life is nonexistent as well." She pulled her keys from her pocket. "I'm leaving. Don't forget Chelsea Waters is coming by tonight to start separating the toys so we know what else we need to purchase with the monetary donations. Please be nice to her."

"Shouldn't you stay to deal with her? After all, this is your idea. I'm just the warehouse." He had no desire to play host to someone, even if it was the founder of Hope's Toy Chest. There were files that required his attention.

"I can't. I told you, Jason and I are leaving early in the morning to drive to his parents' house. I have a ton of things to do. You'll have to deal with it. Give her access if she needs to come back tomorrow." She held up her hand before he could argue. "It's not our fault the warehouse she's been using was sold. She's working on finding somewhere else but it doesn't seem like it will be until after the holidays. So please be nice, this means a lot to me and even more to her. It's only for a bit longer and the holidays will be over and you can have your guest room back so it can gather dust."

He watched his sister stroll out of the house before he let out a deep sigh. Elizabeth always enjoyed Christmas; it had been a season of second chances for her years ago. He never forgot it, but this year even the thought of knowing his sister was with them because of that Christmas miracle couldn't get him out of the funk. He wasn't sure anything could.

The file he had planned to read lay discarded on the kitchen bar. As his discomfort reached an all time high, he decided to step outside. Fresh air would clear his mind of Elizabeth and get him focused on his work again. He grabbed his coat from the hall closet, slipped it on, and buttoned the double-breasted front to keep the chill out.

The snow had begun to fall again, making the twinkling Christmas lights shine brighter. Out of the whole cul-de-sac, his was the only place not decorated. Mentally he made a note to hire someone to revise the issue. This year it might not matter to him, but it mattered to the neighborhood. Their development was known for having the best lit houses at this time of year. People always drove around to look at them. He wouldn't disappoint his neighbors, or the children whose parents drove them through to see the decorations.

Mr. Always Dependable, I guess that describes me to a T.

Letting people down had never been something he was comfortable with. He'd go out of his way to make sure others were happy. Maybe that was why he made such a good doctor. He cared more about his patients than getting home to watch the game, catch a few hours of sleep, or whatever had his fellow colleagues rushing out of the hospital every evening.

Needing to stretch his legs, he wandered around the back of the house leaving footprints in the fresh snow. The back yard was his favorite place. It wasn't because of the pool, it was the view of downtown, the lights twinkling in the distance. Most importantly, the hospital stood tall amongst the others like a beacon guiding him back to where he belonged, back to where people depended on him. The view was the reason he'd bought the house. For some, having a view of their work place would only be a constant reminder of their duties but for him it was a symbol of his accomplishments. All those years of working his ass off had finally paid off. He was doing what he wanted and he made a difference it some people's lives.

The night had chilled too much to stand out there and enjoy it. He shoved his hands into the pockets of his coat with the intent of heading inside, turned around, and walked straight into a woman.

Hope's Toy Chest: Cedar Grove Medical

Chapter Two

He stood there stunned as she fell back into a snow pile. At the last second, he shot an arm out, hoping to catch her, but he was an instant too late.

"I'm sorry, I didn't hear you." He extended a hand, and she took it. He gently pulled her up.

"I called out to you, but I guess you were lost in thought." Her long blonde hair was pulled up in a high ponytail, the curls cascading down her back.

"Are you hurt? I'm so sorry." He cringed, embarrassment overcoming him, his heart pounding as he glanced up and down as if expecting to see blood.

"Nothing's injured but my ego." Her lips curved up, and her green eyes sparkled before she parted her mouth slightly and her smile disappeared. "You're…"

"I'm sorry." He inwardly scolded himself for apologizing three times in less than five minutes; it had to be a record. "I'm Elizabeth's brother Kingsley. I hope she told you she wouldn't be here tonight. They have an early start in the morning to get to her in-laws' house."

"No, you're Doctor Mathews." Tears welled in her eyes, and he began to worry she'd lied about being hurt.

"Umm yes…yes I am." He was suddenly unsure of himself, which was rare. Never before had the mere sight of him sent a woman to tears, and he had no idea how to react, so he just stood there and fidgeted.

"Doctor Mathews." She whispered, more to herself than to him.

"Maybe I should call Elizabeth and she can come over." He stepped back hesitantly, fingering the cell phone in his pocket. Elizabeth was used to dealing with blubbering women; she was a grief counselor at the hospital. He often sent the parents of his patients to her when he could do nothing else for them. He was completely out of his element in a situation like this, especially when he'd done nothing to cause it. At least, he was pretty sure he'd done nothing.

"No, don't bother her. I just need a moment." She ungloved her hand and wiped her eyes.

"Okay, let's get you inside at least. We can't have tears freezing that beautiful face of yours." As he had hoped, that brought a smile to her face. As he led her around the house to the front door, he cursed Elizabeth for leaving him alone. This woman wasn't supposed to be crying, she was only here to separate the toys that cluttered his guest bedroom. Was the thought of all those sick children sending her over the edge?

He urged her to the sofa before dashing into the kitchen for a cup of coffee to warm her up. "Here, drink this." As the steam rose from the big mug, he hoped warmth would bring her out of shock, allowing her to explain what was wrong.

"I'm sorry. I'm not normally like this."

"It's fine." He took a seat on the suede recliner off to the side of the sofa and interlinked his fingers, clutching them together nervously. "If you don't mind me asking, what did I do?"

She squeezed her eyes shut to hold back the tears and took a deep breath before looking up at him. "You treated my daughter. I doubt you remember her." Her voice cracked as she dug through her handbag. "My little redheaded angel, Hope." She handed him a picture.

It was as if a sledgehammer pounded into his chest when he saw the little girl's face. Her death had sent his Christmas spirit crumbling into nothing. Hope Marie Waters. The little girl he lost on Christmas morning two years ago. Everything had been going perfectly with her treatments, and they seemed to be winning the fight against the rare cancer she was battling.

That Christmas morning seemed like any other. It was snowing, which had his spirits high as he made his way across town to Elizabeth and Jason's home, where they always celebrated holiday dinners with their parents, along with Jason's parents and his brother. Three doctors and a grief counselor—it was rare having them all gather together for a meal. It made the holiday even more wonderful, especially to the parents.

The food was spread out across the table and they had just sat down for their early dinner when his cell phone rang. In college he'd been warned he'd always be on call; as a doctor, his time was not his own. That Christmas came the call every doctor dreads. One of his patients needed him. Leaving the meal, he rushed back to the hospital. It was too late.

Looking up from the picture to Chelsea, he instantly recognized her. She was thinner now, but she had the same shimmering green eyes he'd looked into almost every day for nearly two years while Hope fought for her life.

Elizabeth had mentioned Chelsea lost a child to cancer, which was what inspired Hope's Toy Chest, but he'd never put the two together, even considering the timing matched almost perfectly. Hope's Toy Chest had been delivering presents to the Cedar Grove Children's Hospital for the last two years on Christmas. This year it also delivered to some of the sickest children on their birthdays, or whenever they needed something special. All managed by one woman—Chelsea.

"I remember."

"Elizabeth mentioned her brother was a doctor at the hospital, but I never asked anything more. The last names being different I didn't think anything of it. She's married to Doctor Jason West. It's stupid, but I just assumed she was talking about Doctor Brian West."

"A natural assumption. Jason and Brian are both doctors at the hospital, and Jason is a pediatric surgeon while Brian is pediatric cardiologist."

"Then there's Elizabeth dealing with the grieving parents." She shook her head as a strand of hair loosened from her ponytail. "A family surrounded by so much suffering. How do you do it? Or a better question is *why*?"

"We do it for children like Hope. They deserve someone fighting for them."

"There has to be something that led you to your specialty."

"It's a long story." He leaned back in his chair, more content to leave the past where it belonged.

She set the mug aside. "Seems like we have time. According to Elizabeth, I have a room full of toys to go through. If you don't have anything else to do, maybe you'd like to keep me company and tell me about it."

"It's not just my story to tell." That was just an excuse, and he knew it.

"It was a thought. I'm sorry I asked." She stood up, rubbing her hands together as if unsure what to do with herself.

"No, it's okay. I'd just rather not talk about it. I'm not sure Elizabeth would be okay with that." More excuses.

She nodded. "Well, I'd better get busy."

"Your room full of toys is overflowing. I don't think there are enough children in the whole hospital for all that." He took a sip of his coffee.

"There are some children outside the hospital we're delivering to this year as well. If what you say is true, there are going to be some very happy children." She grinned, moving around the sofa. "So where's the stuff?"

"First bedroom on the right. The door's open. Trust me, you can't miss it. You might want to bring them out here to sort and wrap, because you're not going to have room to do it in there." He placed his cup on the table, deciding the files could wait an hour or two. "Would you like some help?"

She smirked. "Sure. Extra hands are good. I never turn them away." Without waiting for him, she strolled down the hall.

He cursed himself for offering to help. There was a little girl depending on him to find a miracle, and he couldn't do that if he was busy wrapping gifts.

She came out with her arms loaded. "You weren't kidding." She placed the toys on the coffee table. "There's so much in there every kid on the list should get what they want. It's going to be a very good Christmas for some deserving children."

"That's wonderful. It makes the unexpected visitors, calls, and packages left on my doorstep worth it."

"I'm sorry. I didn't mean for this to have such an impact on your life. I just don't have room to store it in my small apartment. Elizabeth said you wouldn't mind. How did she *wrap* you into helping anyway? No pun intended."

When she winked, he laughed. "Elizabeth is very good at guilt. Don't get me wrong, I enjoy helping when it comes to wrapping the gifts. I just wasn't completely on board with this taking over my house. I'm rarely home except to sleep, so it just seemed like an additional worry I didn't have time for."

"I'm sorry." She slid a red notebook from her purse, frowning. "I never meant for this to be an inconvenience for you. I had hoped to have a new warehouse by now, but the only place I can find that has the space I need isn't available until after the first of the year."

"It's fine, honestly. There's no reason to move all those toys now."

"Are you sure?" She opened the notebook and set it on the table. "I know it can be a bit much, and you have things that are more important."

"No." He put up a hand to stop her before she could continue. "I believe in what you're doing here. What I said came out wrong." He sat down on the sofa next to where she crouched on the floor and silently berated himself. Chelsea put him on edge for some reason, and he couldn't figure out why. Blaming it on her earlier tears, he pushed forward. "I know what the parents and siblings go through when there's a sick child. This might seem like just presents to some, but it's so much more for those families."

She nodded. "You understand because you work with them each day."

He watched her for a moment before he shook his head.

She twirled her pen in her hand, cocking her head. "Then why? I mean," she shook her head, as if disappointed she couldn't find the right words, and added, "it just seems as if there's more to it than that."

He nodded slowly. "Every time I have to deliver bad news, I...I remember when that same news was handed to my family. So, yes...I understand. Because I know what it's like."

Chapter Three

For the first time in Kingsley's life he wanted to tell someone the whole story. The reason he chose the field he did even with all the pressure, stress, and sadness that it brought him. It was a story he never told anyone. Not even his best friend and colleague Doctor Chaz Romo knew the full story, and they had known each other since medical school.

He patted the seat next to him on the sofa. "Come up here." Pausing while she did so, he tried to put his words together. His thoughts were scattered, setting his nerves off before he even began. What happened to the calm, collected doctor he'd turned himself into over the years?

With more apprehension than he'd ever felt before, he began. "Even with five years separating Elizabeth and I, we're closer than a lot of siblings. We've always been like that." He took her hand into his. It was something he did with families when he was delivering bad news, but this time it was he that sought the comfort of another's touch. Just thinking about the past brought a fresh wave of pain and fear.

"We nearly lost her when she was barely five years old. *Cancer.*" That word tasted rancid on his tongue. "It was sudden and the fight was hard. Many times the doctor told us to prepare for the worse. It was hard on all of us, but I remember sitting by her bed day in and day out, trying to prepare myself for losing her. How does anyone do that?"

She squeezed his hand. "You can't prepare for it. Even though you know the loss is imminent, it just prolongs the grief. You start to grieve for your loved one before you even lose them."

"I couldn't have said it better myself. I remember late at night when I couldn't sleep, I'd sit in Elizabeth's room. Just sitting there surrounded by everything she loved, those horrible pink walls and princess bedspread. Still it brought me comfort." He closed his eyes, and instantly he was ten years old again and back in his sister's room, the grief raw in his chest. "One night Dad found me sitting there, this stupid stuffed penguin in my hands. Elizabeth made a turn for the worst and we rushed back to the hospital. That night was when I decided I'd spend my life searching for a cure. If I could save just one, it would be worth everything."

She squeezed his hand until he looked at her. "A cure always comes with a cost, but look at what progress the medical world has accomplished in the last several years. I believe one day there will be a cure, but something else will replace the disease."

"That's not the world I want to live in. Children shouldn't have to suffer, and they shouldn't be cut down before they have a chance to live." He closed his eyes, letting his anger boil within him. "Aren't you angry Hope couldn't be saved? That I couldn't save her?" That's what it all boiled down to for him. Hope was his responsibility. He'd failed.

"Anger? Yes, I had that, lots of it. In the end I realized nothing could have been done. When someone's time on Earth is over, there's nothing that can be done to stop it. You can't blame yourself, you did everything you could for Hope. If anything, you went above and beyond what was expected of you."

"She was so young."

"Young, but very sick. You did everything you could for her. Don't ever doubt that." She squeezed his hand, giving him reassurance, as he often did with his patients' parents.

"To lose a child is heartbreaking. It makes me reconsider the field I chose." Every time he failed, it ate at him. While he used it to improve, to be ready for it next time, it still caused him to question his career decision.

"Doctor Mathews..."

He stopped her before she could continue. "Kingsley, or Le, please."

"Le, you're an amazing doctor. You care for your patients. I realize that's the downfall as well and could eventually cause you to burn out. You chose pediatric oncology for a reason, and because of that you've saved countless lives. This doubt doesn't stem from not being able to save Hope, does it? I never meant for that."

"No." He pushed off the sofa, needing to do something before he ran his hands through Chelsea's hair. His fingers itched to push the strands away from her face. Confiding in Chelsea had opened him to see her as more than as a former patient's parent. He was seeing her as a woman he wanted to get to know better.

Women were not on the agenda for him. After the hospital, there was nothing left for him to give. There were no hours to devote to a relationship. There was nothing within him when he walked through those doors at the end of the day. A woman, especially Chelsea, deserved better than that. She didn't need someone who would be a daily reminder of Hope and childhood illnesses. Someday she'd put all of this behind her, maybe she'd even distance herself from the organization and allow others to handle it so she could have a life beyond cancer.

"Then what brought this up?"

He dragged his hand over his face. "I have a little girl under my care, and it's unlikely she'll see Christmas, okay? I'm furious, damn it!" He wanted to slam his fist through a wall. Instead he clenched his fingers together and stared down at the floor.

She stood, tentatively came to him, and placed her hand on his arm. "I'm sorry."

"No, I'm sorry. You're here to go through the toys, not listen to my problems." He forced a smile. "Come on, let's see what we've got for the children."

"I understand if you need to work. I can do this."

"Work?" He tried to laugh, but even to his own ears it was halfhearted. "You mean the file I bought home that I was going to read for the hundredth time? There's nothing new added to it. If you weren't here, I'd spend the night going over each report until my eyes bled and still have no miracle for her." When she raised an eyebrow at him, he took her hand in his. "This is a much better way to spend the evening. So tell me what I can do to help."

Nodding, she turned around and grabbed the notebook. "We have more toys than I expected, and it's going to take me some time to go through all of them. This is the worst part of not having a warehouse. I have no space to divide them up."

"Use whatever space you need, just leave me a path to my bed and you can spread things out everywhere else."

"Oh no, I couldn't do that."

"Why not? I don't use the house for anything but a few hours of sleep." He stepped around her, moving back over to the kitchen bar to where the key hook was mounted. He snatched a key off the peg. "Here."

"What's this for?"

"It's a key, you're welcome here anytime. Just lock up when you leave." For a moment he wondered if he was doing the right thing, giving his house key to a woman he barely knew.

"This isn't necessary." She reasoned as he pressed the key into her palm.

"Actually it is." He held her hand longer than necessary, enjoying the feeling of her warmth. "With my hours at the hospital, and emergencies, I can never be sure when I'm home. You need access to the toys in order to divide them and get them ready for delivery. I'll help with whatever I can, but you still need to be able to get through all of them and that's going to take time. More time than you have tonight."

"Thank you. I'll do my best so that it doesn't interfere with your life."

He wanted to laugh at the comment. He didn't have a life outside of his duties, there was only work.

"How many children are on your list?" he asked.

"Eighty-four. This year we extended beyond the children with grave prognoses." She flipped open the notebook.

"That's it?" His eyes widened at the thought of how many toys cluttered his spare bedroom. There was more than what was needed for eighty-four children, so what would she do with the rest?

"Yeah. We were open to a hundred children this year and we were close, but some of them transferred to other hospitals, went into remission, or... You know." She didn't have to say some of them didn't make it, because he already knew. It was the cost of their work, they had to face the sadness of death often.

"Aren't there too many toys then?"

"Our biggest drive is right before Christmas, so whatever's left over we use for gifts throughout the year for children's birthdays, pick me ups, and so on. But don't worry, I'll get them out of your house after the holidays." She sat back down on the sofa. "I have the wish list for each of the children in my notebook. I'll do my best to match the toys in your bedroom to the children. Whatever I don't have I can use the monetary donations to purchase."

"Well, what can I do to help?"

"I grabbed these because I know they are on the list. Can you bring another armload out? I'll start going through them. I'll need to make piles for each of the children. Are you sure you don't mine me taking over your house? I'll try to limit it to the bedroom and here."

He shook his head. "It's fine. The only place that's off limits is my office so I can get some work done when I'm here if I need to."

"I'll stay out of those rooms." She turned to the first child on the list. "You don't have a tree up yet, should I leave you space for it?"

"Don't worry about it."

"Everyone needs a tree…"

"I'm never here, and on Christmas I'll be at Elizabeth's anyway."

She shrugged and turned to her list. He looked around his living room and hated how dull it seemed. There was nothing that said Christmas, and it was only a few weeks away. He couldn't muster up the energy to decorate. After all, he was broken inside. Christmas decorations couldn't fix that.

Hope's Toy Chest: Cedar Grove Medical

Chapter Four

Kingsley slowly made his way through the hospital lobby, exhaustion clinging to him as it never had before. He usually fell asleep within seconds, but last night after Chelsea had left, he spent the night tossing and turning. The sandman never visited him.

"Damn, man, you look like shit, as if you've been here all night or something." His brother-in-law Jason stepped up beside him.

"Not all of us have Liz to take care of us. Why are you here anyway? I thought you and Liz were driving up to your parents' house."

"I got called in around one this morning, an emergency surgery." He dragged his hand over his face. "A seven-year-old boy was sleep walking and stepped right out of his house and into oncoming traffic. It was a mess."

"Is he going to make it?"

Jason nodded. "I think so, and it will be a miracle. He was a mess when they brought him in, but somehow he's made it through the surgery and his vitals look good. It's a damn miracle he made it to the hospital, let alone lived this long. The boy's a fighter."

"Any lasting trauma?"

"We had no choice but to amputate his leg below the knee." Jason slipped his stethoscope from around his neck and shoved it in his pocket. "It's Christmas and what does the boy get…his damn leg amputated."

"I know it's no comfort, but it could be worse. At least the family still has their son."

"You're right. The mother didn't care about anything except he survived. The father wanted to know what kind of normal life his son would lead with half a leg missing." Jason shoved his hands into his pocket. "Sorry to burden you with this, you've got enough on your plate. I've got to go, Elizabeth is waiting at home for us to head out."

"Have a safe trip." He said his goodbyes and stepped onto the elevator. There was one little girl that was going to be his first stop. He needed to see how she was doing before he continued on to his office.

The hours of sleeplessness had left him with no new revelations as to what might help his patient. Christmas was right around the corner and if there was going to be a miracle, this was the time of year for it. He slipped his coat off just as the elevator doors opened.

"Doctor Mathews." The nurse behind the desk looked up from the file she was making notations in and called to him.

"Morning, Nancy."

"Jessica's mother asked to speak to you when you arrived. If you want to go to your office, I can show her the way."

"Any change in Jessica's condition?" He knew asking was pointless. The nurses had orders to contact him immediately if there was any change.

With sadness in her eyes, Nancy shook her head. They had all been down this road countless times, but it never got easier. "She's sleeping peacefully at the moment."

He tossed his coat on the nurse's counter. "I'll check in on them, and pick this up on my way through."

"Very well, Doctor Mathews." She turned her attention back to the file in her hand.

The hard soles of his dress shoes clicked against the tiled floor like the ringing of doom. Jessica's mother, Kelly, was holding out hope. Each day she wanted to know if anything had changed in her daughter's prognosis, and each day he had to tell her the same thing.

Without entering, he paused by the door, glancing in the hall window at the sleeping little girl and Kelly sitting by her bedside looking completely exhausted. It still bothered him that the nurse, Patsy, thought it was better for the mother to lose her only child. Sure she could have more children, but no one would ever replace her first daughter. Jessica was a fighter. She never complained, no matter how sick she was, and there was always a smile on her face. She was truly a happy child.

As if she felt his gaze, Kelly's eyes opened. She glanced to her daughter before stepping out in the hall to join him. "I'd like a moment to talk to you alone, but I don't want to leave her," she whispered, her voice strained.

"Nancy can sit with her for a moment if you'd like, and we can go to my office." When she nodded, he called for Nancy. "I need a moment with Mrs. Cook, if you could sit with Jessica."

"It would be my pleasure." Nancy smiled, and went to join the sleeping child.

"This way." He grabbed his jacket off the counter before leading her down the hallway. His office was just at the end of the hall, close to his patients and their families.

"Thank you for taking the time to speak with me this morning."

"I'm always here." He pushed open the door, holding it open for her to enter. "Please have a seat and tell me what I can do for you." He hung up his coat on the peg by the door and made his way over to her. He didn't bother going behind the heavy mahogany desk. Instead, he took a seat next to her in one of the plush chairs.

"Last night was a rough night for Jessica. The radiation made her extremely ill." She wiped her hands on her pants.

"We spoke about this before. If we stop her radiation treatments, her prognosis becomes dire. It is your choice, but I would strongly advise against it." He knew how rough the radiation was, especially at the level they were doing it, but it was the only thing that *might* help. Even then it would only prolong the inevitable; they had no cure.

"That's not why I asked to meet with you." She leaned forward, placing her elbows on her knees. "Tomorrow is her third treatment, then she has a day off before the next three days of radiation. I want to take her home."

"Mrs. Cook…"

She put up her hand stopping him. "Please just hear me out." When he nodded, she continued. "Just for a few hours…we both know it's doubtful she'll make it until Christmas. Let me take her home and give her a proper Christmas. I can have my sister come in, clean, and put up the Christmas tree."

"You know if Jessica leaves the hospital, it's likely she'll catch a virus, her frail body couldn't handle that now. It's too much of a risk."

"If this is her last Christmas, I want to make it memorable. Please, Doctor Mathews, there's got to be something you can do." Tears glistened in Kelly's eyes as she begged him to give her daughter one final Christmas celebration. "Please…"

Hope's Toy Chest: Cedar Grove Medical

Chapter Five

Kingsley sat at his desk long after Mrs. Cook had left, trying to figure out a way to make her wish come true. She wasn't asking too much by wanting to have a semblance of normalcy for their last Christmas together. Now he just had to figure out a way to do it without risking his patient.

Suddenly he shot from his chair, nearly spilling his coffee over everything. If he could get the approval of the Hospital Administrator, he might be able to make a special Christmas for Jessica after all. That and a little help from Chelsea. He finished off his coffee and headed for the door. Calling might have saved him time if Doctor Annabell Booth was busy, but he needed to stretch his legs.

Doctors, nurses, patients, and families moved quickly through the long corridors of the hospital, each rushing to and from. It always surprised him how many emotions could be seen throughout a hospital. Families receiving good news glowed with a fresh start, while others had unshed tears glistening in their eyes.

With his mind elsewhere, he quickly made his way through the hospital, and up to the eighth floor where the administration offices were. Stepping off the elevator, he found Grace sitting behind her desk. Grace had worked for the hospital for over twenty years, her salt and pepper hair in a fashionable bob cut, her business suit perfectly pressed. The way she glanced up from behind her glasses made him feel like he was back in school again.

"Doctor Mathews, how can I help you?" Grace had known him when he was just a boy, visiting his sister. Back then, she had been a nurse on Elizabeth's floor. They had kept in touch and when he graduated medical school, she had been there, beaming from ear to ear.

"I was hoping to have a minute of Doctor Booth's time. It's somewhat of an urgent matter."

"Ahh, now that might be a problem. She had a very busy schedule today." While Grace glanced at the schedule, he waited, not at all surprised Annabell was busy. She was even more of a workaholic than him, if that was even possible. Annabell had been the Chief of the Emergency Room before going over to the dark side—administration. She had always played well with others and with her experience and knowledge she made an excellent Hospital Administrator.

"I'll make myself available whenever she can squeeze me in and I promise I only need five minutes of her time."

"She's got a few minutes before her next appointment, let me see if she can talk now as a favor to me. I know you wouldn't be here in person without calling ahead if it wasn't important." She stood from her desk. "No promises."

"Thank you." He was grateful for her kindness.

He slipped his hand into the pocket of his dress slacks and fingered his cell phone, trying to determine when Elizabeth and Jason would make it through the bad reception area. She'd have a phone number for Chelsea, but a trip home, with lunch for the two of them, might be the better way to convince her that he needed her help. He tried not to think about the fact that she had occupied the majority of his thoughts since she left.

Grace stepped out of the office, drawing his attention. "You've got three minutes."

"I owe you." He stepped around her, nearing the door. "Thank you."

Stepping into the office, he found Annabell sitting behind the desk, looking both tired and ready to take on whatever scumbag who wanted to cheat the patients from their health benefits. "Thank you for taking the time to see me. I understand you're busy and only need a moment."

She leaned back in her leather chair, a pen still in hand, and glanced up at him. "Sit down and get to it, Kingsley."

"A no-nonsense woman, I like that." He teased, taking a seat in front of her desk.

"Your flirting will get you nowhere with me. Those big blue eyes don't work on me like they do on Grace." She gave him a smile.

She had a way of putting everyone at ease. She was a strict boss, but fair. "Fine then, I'll cut to it. One of my patients isn't going to make it to the holidays and I was hoping to do something special for her."

"I'm listening."

"Jessica has been in and out of the hospital since she was nine months old. Five long years of treatments, needles, and endless hospital stays." He paused for a moment before leaning forward. "At one time the ninth floor was used as rooms for the parents, or those traveling through. I know we still have the rooms for medical students, and other staff if they need a crash room when working long hours."

"Don't forget the storage," she reminded him. "Now how about you tell me what you're getting at?"

"Jessica's mother wants to take her out of the hospital, the day after tomorrow, to have one final Christmas with her that isn't surrounded by the nursing staff, doctors, machines, and the sickly scent of bleach. I can't with good conscious sign off on it. Jessica is in too frail of health to risk her catching a virus, traveling in this weather." He took a deep breath, his breath caught in his throat. "I want to take over one of the rooms and give Jessica the Christmas she deserves. To let them spend the night there with the Christmas decorations, and the next morning can be their Christmas, and Jessica can open her presents."

"You don't think it would be too much for her?"

"She'd be in a safe and secure environment. I'll stay here at the hospital, checking in on her to make sure everything is fine. If there are any changes in her health, I'll return her to the floor. She's on a three day radiation with one day off rotation. The day after tomorrow is her off day."

"How are you going to pull this off by yourself?" She tossed her pen on the desk, watching him.

"I know someone who'd be willing to help, and Elizabeth will be back in town that morning. If there are any last minute things, I know I can count on her and Jason. Do I have your approval?"

"To take a sick child up there you're going to need a deep cleaning of the room."

"I won't ask for the hospital cleaners. I'll see to it and everything else. Cleaning, decorations, everything. What do you say?" His stomach churned waiting for the answer. It was worse than waiting to see if he'd gotten into his top choice for medical school.

She nodded. "Don't take any unnecessary risks with her health."

Excitement coursed through him, and for that brief moment the joys of Christmas began to return to him. "Thank you."

He stood and quickly made his way to the door. There was so much to do before Jessica's Christmas celebration. The first thing he needed to do was talk to Chelsea.

Hope's Toy Chest: Cedar Grove Medical

Chapter Six

Chelsea sat in the middle of Kingsley's living room surrounded by mountains of toys. Thanks to his key, she'd been able to make a dent, as small as it might be. She had managed to get the stuff divided for two children. Now she sat there wrapping them, putting them in a Santa sack to be delivered on Christmas Eve.

The front door opened, and dress shoes made a dull thud on the hardwood floor. "Chelsea?"

"In here." She put the last piece of tape on the baby doll and tossed it onto the pile in the sack. "What brings you home at this time of the day?"

"Lunch." He held up a bag of Chinese food. "Want to join me?"

With a glance at the clock, she smirked. "It's ten-thirty in the morning. Where did you find a Chinese restaurant open at this time?"

"The one by the hospital is always open early preparing for the day. They'll take orders from us at the hospital before they open." He set the bag on the table. "I thought we could have some lunch and I could convince you to help a little girl."

"You didn't have to bribe me. After all, I owe you for letting me take over your house." She stood up, carefully making her way through the piles. "It smells delicious."

"I'll grab plates and we can talk about what I'd like your help with." He turned to the cherry wood cabinets and grabbed the dishes. "I got chicken and broccoli, beef teriyaki, and crab rangoon."

"Can I get drinks?"

"I keep a pitcher of water with a splash of lemon in the refrigerator. If you'd like to pour me a glass, I'd appreciate it." He took the dishes to table and begun unwrapping the food. "You mentioned expanding Hope's Toy Chest. Well, I have a new idea."

"You didn't even wait until you've plied me with good food before you jump right into what you need from me." She brought the drinks over and sat down. "So get on with it."

She took a drink, and one of the crab rangoons, before looking up at him. The idea of expanding Hope's Toy Chest brought a new level of excitement to her. The organization in her daughter's memory had become her coping mechanism and her life. There was nothing outside of the organization for her, at least nothing since her divorce. Her and her husband didn't make it a year after Hope's death before their divorce proceedings started. Without Hope they had nothing left between them, and there seemed to be no point in staying together.

"The little girl I mentioned last night who's dying. I need your help to bring her a Christmas the day after tomorrow."

"Season of miracles, but I think we can pull it off. A Christmas in her hospital room?" She accepted her food and dug in.

"The hospital used to have guest rooms on the ninth floor for the families of the sickest children, or those traveling through. Now they are just used for medical students and crash rooms when working doubles. I've got permission to take over one of those rooms to give her a good celebration. The plan is to take her up tomorrow evening. She'll go to bed with a Christmas tree shining bright, and when she wakes up Santa—well, us—will have delivered her gifts."

"Can you get me a list of what she'd like? I'll gather it, and wrap it." She took a bite of chicken.

"I'll speak with her mother. If you're willing to help, I'll get everything else lined up." He began eating his own meal.

"What's everything else?"

"I need to have the room sanitized, then decorated. That reminds me, if you hear people outside this afternoon, it's nothing. I hired people to come decorate. I've got an image to uphold with my neighbors, can't let the children down just because I've lost the spirit."

"How about we try to regain that spirit of the holidays by decorating the hospital room ourselves? We can do it this evening once you're done working. I can get the decorations and meet you there." She pushed the broccoli aside.

"Didn't your mother teach you that you should eat your vegetables? It will keep the doctors away." He teased.

"I eat salads, cucumbers, peppers, and fruits. A little vegetable neglect won't kill me." She didn't want to keep the doctor away; neglecting all her fruit and vegetables might keep him around longer.

He let out a lighthearted chuckle. "You don't have to decorate. I know you have enough to deal with."

"I don't mind. I was just sitting in your living room thinking you needed a tree as well."

"I just haven't been in the mood this season. It seems to have lost its joy." With his plate now cleaned, he sat his fork down. "I have a meeting with a parent to discuss treatment options at four-thirty, so how about you meet me at the hospital at six?"

"That will be fine. Are you going to be able to get it cleaned before then?"

"I'm going to call my housekeeper, and see if she can do it for me today." He slipped his phone from his pocket. "I should do that and then get back to the hospital."

"Go ahead. I'll clean up."

He took his plate to the sink and rinsed it before putting it in the dishwasher. "Sorry to rush off." When she waved his apology away, he slipped his jacket on. "I'll have a list of stuff for you tonight. After we decorate, maybe we can get some dinner and come back here to find the stuff on her wish list," he suggested.

Dinner with him seemed more intimate and sent butterflies spinning within her. "That would be nice."

"Very well. In the closet of my office are the Christmas decorations I have. Help yourself to anything we might need."

"Thanks, but you're going to need them here. Plus I keep extra supplies around just for cases like this." She finished off the last crab rangoon and watched him walk out the door. He could fill out those dress slacks like no other man she knew. She wanted to touch him, to feel his body beneath her fingers.

She closed her eyes, letting the fantasy take hold. It had been so long since she felt anything stir within her. Letting her mind wander to what he might look like under those clothes, how his body would feel pressed against her.

He's not the type of man to get involved with, even in my fantasies.

Kingsley was dedicated to his work, and she wasn't sure she could take the backseat to his career. When her divorce was finalized, she'd promised herself that if she ever got involved again it would be with someone who would love her for who she was, not who she could be or what she could do for them. She had spent too long as the woman on her husband's arm, and then the perfect housewife while her husband was busy with his career. Never again.

Hope's Toy Chest: Cedar Grove Medical

Chapter Seven

Kingsley had everything in order for the celebration for the Cook family. The only thing left was the decorations and the presents. Hope's Toy Chest would be providing some of the toys, and Kelly's sister would be bringing the ones they had purchased in the morning. Little Jessica was going to have a Christmas that would make other children envious.

It was only five-thirty but he figured he'd mosey down to the lobby and help Chelsea carry the decorations in. He shut down his computer and went to grab his jacket when a knock sounded at his door.

"Come in."

Grace opened the door and peaked her head in. "I was hoping I'd catch you here. Annabell told me of your plans and I wanted to offer Tony's services to you. He plays Santa for the ward parties, and a couple events. He could stop by Jessica's room before she goes to bed. Jessica with Santa in front of the tree would be a good photo for Kelly, one that she'd hold dear always."

"Are you sure Tony won't mind? I don't know why I didn't think of that before."

"No, he'd love to."

"Perfect. We're moving her upstairs around seven."

"Good. I'll have him here at six-thirty to make sure she's still awake."

"Thank you, Grace, and tell Tony I owe him one."

"We're glad to do it. This is a great thing you're doing for the Cooks. If you need anything, just let me know."

He curved his lips into a smile, knowing she had a hard time saying no to him. "Actually, now that you mention it, there's something else. On Jessica's off days from radiation, she has a sweet tooth, and she loves chocolate cake. It's so much better when it's homemade instead of what I could buy. What do you say?"

With a quick nod, she turned to leave. "I'll make her my triple chocolate cake and bring it tomorrow night. See you then."

"Thank you." He called after her before grabbing his coat. He didn't slip it on, but instead slung it over his arm.

For the first time in months, he strolled out of his office in a good mood. He left his worries behind him, and looked forward to the evening activates. Decorating the room upstairs held more appeal to him than decorating his own house, because tomorrow evening he'd be able to see Jessica's face when they revealed what they'd pulled together for her. That in itself made everything worth it.

"Doctor Mathews." Nancy hollered to him just before he stepped into the elevator. "Can I have a moment?"

"Everything okay?" He glanced at his watch.

"I heard what you're doing for the Cooks and I'd like to volunteer to stay over tomorrow to look after Jessica."

"That's appreciated but not necessary. I'll be staying upstairs."

"I understand but I would still like to help. Jessica has captured all our hearts, and I would love to be a part of this special celebration for her."

"Very well. The accommodations are rough, but we'll only be there one night, and like you said it will be worth it. I'll see you tomorrow night at six o'clock, so we can take her upstairs around seven. We'll give them most of the next day and bring her back onto the ward that evening. You don't have to stay the whole time."

"I'll be there. Thank you." She went back to the nurse's desk.

Nancy had lost a child years ago, not because of cancer but a freak accident. It gave her an insight to just what the parents were going through. She might be a comfort to Kelly. As he waited for the elevator, he had a moment to realize how amazing his team was. His staff always rallied together when something needed to be done. It made him feel good to work with such a wonderful team of caring professionals.

The elevator doors opened and there stood Chelsea, her arms loaded with bags. "I managed everything but the tree."

"Let me take some of that." He grabbed some of the bags from her, lightening her load. "You shouldn't have brought all this at once. I was coming down to help." He hit the button for the ninth floor.

"I figured there wasn't a reason to make a dozen trips. Taking all this now means we only have one trip left. The tree is stored in two smaller boxes, so we can both go grab one and be done. Were you able to get the list?"

"It's in my jacket pocket but I can't get to it now." He smirked at them both standing there with their arms loaded. "I don't think I have this much stuff for my whole house."

"I'm not surprised, you're a man. Women go all out. It's going to be a Christmas wonderland for her. I assumed we couldn't have a live tree, but we are going to make up for it with the decorations."

"Live trees are out of the question. I should have mentioned that."

"Nothing to worry about, I told you I had this part covered." She adjusted her armful before stepping off the elevator. "Did you get the place cleaned?"

"My housekeeper left about forty minutes ago. She did a good job, not that I expected anything less. She's always very thorough. She made up both of the beds in the room with fresh sheets, as well as the room next to it where I'll be spending the night to supervise Jessica's health."

"You're staying?"

"With her not being on the ward, there's no nurses to watch over her. Nancy—the head nurse of the oncology floor—has offered to stay over as well. We'll be able to take turns checking in on Jessica." He nodded up the hall. "Second door on the right."

They stepped into a room that was larger than most double occupancy hospital rooms. There were four beds, two on each side, with big windows along the wall that could get a lot of light in the day, or could be closed off with darkening shades for sleep.

"This is bigger than I expected, I might need more decorations."

He set everything he had been carrying on the floor. "No."

"That sounds like a man who *thinks* he's in charge." She dropped her stuff as well and then sat down on the edge of one of the unmade beds.

"Thinks?" He raised an eyebrow at her, trying to keep his mind away from his fantasy—pushing her back on the bed, exploring every curve of her body.

"Oh yes, thinks." She leaned back on the bed, propping herself up on her elbows. "After all, you brought this to me, asked for my help, and suggested this would be a great expansion for Hope's Toy Chest. That makes *me* in charge, and if I say more decorations then more is what we need. I won't be outdone on this celebration. Now come on, let's see if you can make yourself useful and help me decorate."

"You better be glad Elizabeth likes you." He teased. "You start going through this stuff and I'll get the tree." Needing to get away before he lost control of himself, he turned on his heels.

She was the parent of a former patient, one he couldn't save, and he couldn't get involved with her. No matter how attractive he might find her, or how his body called to her. He could never put his career on the back burner, and she deserved more than that. She deserved someone who would be home with her for dinner each night, someone who could give her time and commitment, show her how wonderful she was. She couldn't get involved with a doctor, someone who would never have time outside the hospital.

But no matter, what he couldn't stop thinking about her and it was beginning to drive him a little crazy. He'd never been so preoccupied with anything other than his work.

Focus on Jessica, and keep your mind off Chelsea.

Easier said than done.

Chapter Eight

Kingsley tossed the empty pizza box in the trash before leaning against the counter. It had been a long time since he made his way over to D's Pizza. Their square pizza by the slice with the thick, crunchy, crust was heavenly. After spending nearly three hours at the hospital decorating the room to perfection, there had been little choice but to grab pizza and come back to his place.

"I can't remember ever having such delicious pizza. Wow. I don't even like crust normally." Chelsea sat there at the table looking as if she was in Heaven.

"It's sure worth the twenty minute drive." He stepped away from the counter and added more wine to their glasses. The desire to move into the living room, curl up with a beautiful woman and a good movie was new to him. Over the years there had been flings, but no one ever made him feel like he did in that moment. She occupied his thoughts, even when she wasn't physically there, and the longing to touch her was almost overpowering.

A little voice inside him reminded him of Hope, screaming for him to make an excuse to go to his office and busy himself with work. He couldn't get involved with her, no matter how much he wanted her. He tried to force his thoughts back to the duty ahead; they still had to find the toys from Jessica's wish list and wrap them.

"We should start…"

"There's time." He sat down next to her, not wanting the moment to end. "You're a big reason why this is possible for Jessica."

"You're the one doing it. I just provided the decorations."

"The presents as well," he reminded her. "What I'm saying is that I'd like to invite you to be there. You won't want to stay in those shitty crash rooms, but you can come by in the morning to see her with the gifts."

"Oh no, I wouldn't want to intrude. This is a celebration for Jessica and her mother."

"That's your choice. Will you join us tomorrow evening? Santa will be making a visit, maybe you can ask him for your own Christmas wish."

"Okay. That sounds like fun, but does Santa still deliver to old women?"

"You're not old." He slipped his hand over hers. What he really wanted to say was how beautiful she was. "Santa will make a special delivery for you if you tell him what you want."

"I'll be sure to do that. It would be nice to be on the receiving end for once." She blushed, taking a sip of her wine. "Now come on, we've got to find the stuff on the list if either of us is going to get some sleep."

They rose from the table but before they could move away from it, his cell phone went off. "Excuse me a moment." He grabbed the phone from the counter. "Doctor Mathews."

"Doctor, this is Tammy, a R.N. at Cedar Grove Children's Hospital. There's a note here that you want to be notified of any changes in Jessica Cook's condition."

"Yes, how is she?"

"She spiked a fever and has become violently ill. As stated in her chart, we administered the medication through her IV." The nurse rambled on, the lack of feeling in her voice bothering him, making him wonder if she wasn't in the wrong field.

"How long has she been showing symptoms? Any change since the medication was given?"

"She received the first dose just over an hour ago and no changes as of yet."

He gulped, a cold sweat passing over him. "Give her a second dose and I'll be in." He glanced at the clock. "Twenty minutes."

"I don't believe that's necessary."

"I do." He emptied his wine glass into the sink. "With her current condition I'd like to examine her." Without waiting for her reply, he ended the call and glanced to where Chelsea stood waiting for him.

"The hospital?" She frowned.

Her expression reminded him why relationships never lasted for him. He had yet to find a woman who would understand his career, and he doubted he ever would. "I'm afraid so. Jessica's taken a turn, and I need to go check on her."

"Go ahead. If you don't mind, I'll stay and find what we need for tomorrow."

"Hopefully tomorrow is still doable."

"That bad?"

He prayed not, but there was only one way to find out. He stepped toward her and took her hand in his. "I don't know how long I'll be. If you're gone by the time I get back I'll give you a call in the morning to let you know if we're still on for the celebration."

"Go, she needs you."

He wanted to kiss her, to ask her to stay, instead he grabbed his coat and headed for the door. There would be another night for them. Jessica, on the other hand, might only have a few hours left.

The minutes ticked by and still Chelsea stood in the middle of Kingsley's kitchen, her mind on his touch. The brief moments when their hands met sent her heart fluttering. She had never been drawn to someone the way she was drawn to Le. For the first time she was seeing him in a new light. When he was her daughter's doctor, she didn't see him, not really. He was just there; her daughter had been at the forefront of things, and everything else was just background. Now she could see he was so much more than just a doctor. He truly cared for his patients, and he grieved for those he'd lost as much as the families did. Le was a man who would never be satisfied until childhood cancer was a thing of the past, until he was put out of a job because of a cure.

Having been in the position of the parents with sick children she knew just how valuable a dedicated doctor was. Le had done his best to help her daughter. He had done everything that could be done. Even at the very end, when they knew the time was coming, he had been there. Thinking back, she remembered him always being present. She never realized it then, but even late at night when Hope had gotten worse, he had been there.

Throughout it all, he had a word of encouragement when she needed it, a tissue when there was nothing to say. When Hope lost her fight, he had rushed to the hospital, arriving only minutes after she died, and held her while she cried. He had come to the funeral, offering his help with anything she needed, going above and beyond what was expected of him.

Knowing how dedicated he was to his career and patients, she still couldn't stop herself from wanting him. He had a heart of gold, and the body of a god. A flush of heat washed through her. Damn, did she want him.

Would Santa bring her a second chance at love?

Hope's Toy Chest: Cedar Grove Medical

Chapter Nine

It was after two in the morning when Kingsley opened the door to his house. The only thing on his mind was sleep. They had finally brought down Jessica's fever and she was resting comfortably, on oxygen to help her breathe, and additional antibiotics to combat the slight congestion in her lungs. Stepping inside, he slipped out of his coat. The living room light glowed through the darkness, and there on the sofa Chelsea was sound asleep.

He hung his coat in the hall closet before strolling into the living room. A beautiful woman waiting for him when he got home made his heart skip a beat. If only he could pick her up and carry her to his bed, feel her warm body pressed against his. He needed to put distance between them or he was going to end up breaking her heart.

Even knowing that, he couldn't stop his body from moving forward. He leaned over the sofa, rubbing his finger along her jawline. "Chelsea." Oh, how he loved the way her name rolled off his tongue.

A soft moan escaped her lips as she turned her face into his hand, her eyes still closed. "Hmm."

"Come on, sweetie, wake up." He dragged his hand through her hair, the soft strands sliding through his fingers like silk.

Her eyelids shot open. "I'm sorry, I didn't mean to fall asleep." She rubbed her hand over her face.

"It's fine, and it's late. The snow has started and the roads are getting bad. Why don't you stay here tonight?"

"The same bedroom we have a million toys piled into?" She scooted up on the sofa, pulling her legs under her.

"I do have another guest room, come on. It's late and you need some sleep." He took her hand in his. "It's too nasty for you to go out in this storm." He led her down the hall toward the guest room closest to his. Everything within him screamed for him to take her to his bed, even if it was only for one night.

She leaned against him, half asleep, as he pushed the bedroom door open. "Thank you." Her words came out in a soft whisper. "You don't have to be so nice to me."

"Yeah, let me just throw you out on a cold and snowy night, that's what a gentleman would do." He led her to the bed, and pulled down the comforter. "Get into bed, we'll talk in the morning."

"Okay." She mumbled, climbing into bed with her clothes on. The minute her head hit the pillow she was asleep.

With her snuggly under the blankets, he made his way to his room. He needed to get a few hours of sleep and get back to the hospital to check on Jessica and his other patients. There was also a stack of paperwork that needed to be completed by week's end if he didn't want the hospital administration staff and Annabell breathing down his neck. He pushed it aside and slipped between the sheets, his mind wandering back to Chelsea.

Kingsley awoke to screams and shot out of bed. It was the middle of the night, darkness enveloped his house, but he knew something had woken him and he wasn't sure where it had come from. In an instant, he knew.

"Hope!" Chelsea's terrified voice cut through the stillness of the night.

He rushed to the door, not bothering to grab any clothes. Something was wrong. Dashing down the hall, he pushed open the door. There in the middle of the bed, Chelsea struggled against the tangled sheets.

"God, no, Hope!"

"Sweetie." He closed the distance to the bed and wrapped his arms around her, pulling her close to him. She fought against him, tears pouring down her face. "Chels, it's okay. I've got you."

"No, please." Her fists slammed into him.

"Come on, wake up." He leaned against the pillows, holding her to him, and running his hands down her arms. "Chels."

"Hope." Finally waking, her voice was cloaked with tears, and she clung to him.

They sat there as he gently caressed her until the tears finally ended. "Are you okay?" She nodded, her body shaking like a leaf. "Do you want to talk about it?"

She laced her fingers through his. "Hope…she came to me in the dream."

He nodded, resting his cheek against the top of her head. "You were screaming her name."

"She came to me, and she'll come for Jessica."

Knowing it was a dream didn't stop him from feeling sick. He didn't want to lose another child, not at Christmas, not ever. "It was only a dream." He was trying to reassure them both.

"It seemed liked so much more than that." She curled into him until they were looking at each other. "We've got to do something."

"I'm doing everything I can." He held her, needing to feel her against him, grounding him.

"I know you are." Tears cascaded over her cheeks. "That poor mother."

Somewhere in the midst of all of it, beyond the sadness and helplessness, he realized he was falling for her. It was a whole new territory for him, one he wasn't sure she was the perfect person to explore it with. He still wasn't sure what she saw or felt when she looked at him. Did she see someone that had failed her? Would they be able to use that as the foundation to a relationship instead of a divider?

"I'm sorry." She wiped her eyes, drying the tears.

"There's nothing to be sorry about, nightmares happen."

"This wasn't just a nightmare, this was a warning. Is Jessica's mother ready for what's coming? Is there anything I can do?"

"No one is ever ready. She's holding out hope, but I think she realizes it's a possibility or she wouldn't have wanted to celebrate Christmas early." He brushed the hair away from her cheek.

"You're right, you're never ready to lose a child." Her hair tickled his chest when she nodded.

"Things were different in your case. Hope's change was quick and unexpected. Jessica hasn't had any positive reactions to *any* treatments she has undergone."

He was prepared for failing Jessica. He'd done everything he could, even used experimental treatments, and nothing had worked. Losing Hope had been a surprise. She had been on her way to recovery, the treatment had been working for her.

A sudden change and everything had gone wrong.

Hope's Toy Chest: Cedar Grove Medical

Chapter Ten

Chelsea put the final touches on the hospital room. In just a few minutes, Le would be bringing Jessica and her mother up, and she wanted everything to be prefect. She plugged in the tree, letting the warm white lights cast a glow over the space. This had to be perfect, because it would be one of the last memories of mother and daughter together, one she knew Mrs. Cook would always cherish.

Hearing the faint ding of the elevator, she quickly grabbed the two gift boxes she'd brought with her that afternoon and placed them by the tree. They were gifts that could be opened before Santa's visit. It was a tradition she had as a child, and one she continued with Hope. Now she was sharing it with the Cooks.

Le pushed a wheelchair through the door, the IV bag reminding her just how sick Jessica was. "Jessica, this is a friend of mine, Chelsea."

"I've heard so much about you." Kelly stepped around Le and held out her hand. "Thank you for everything."

Chelsea took the offered hand with a smile. "There's no need for that, I'm glad to help."

"Mommy, look, a Christmas tree!" Jessica appeared so frail curled up in the wheelchair, thick blankets tucked around her. Her bald head served as a reminder of just how sick she was, but despite her illness the sight of the decorations made her blue eyes glisten with excitement.

"I see, sweetie." She returned to her daughter's side, taking the blanket from her lap as Le lifted Jessica into the bed they had made up for her. "Can you tell Doctor Mathews and Chelsea thank you for setting this up?"

"Thank you." Her small hand covered her mouth as a coughing fit followed, but her eyes were wide with delight as she looked around the room. "Is it really Christmas tomorrow?"

"For us it is." Kelly sat on the edge of the bed, her daughter's hand in hers.

"I hope you don't mind, but growing up I had a special tradition." Chelsea grabbed the gift boxes and handed the smaller one to Jessica, giving the other one to Kelly. "Merry Christmas."

"Can I open it?" Jessica bounced on her bed, clearly excited.

"Go ahead." Kelly nodded, slipping the lid off her own box, while Jessica tore through the wrapping paper. Matching red satin pajamas with white trim for their Christmas Eve together. "Oh, they're beautiful." Kelly's eyes watered.

"Growing up, my parents started this tradition to have new pajamas on Christmas Eve. It was the one present we were allowed to open early," she explained.

"We'll let you change and settle in." Le nodded to the door and Chelsea made her way to him. "I've got a special visitor coming soon, so until I get back I want you to rest."

"Yes, doctor." Jessica smiled at him, running her hands over her new pajamas.

"I'm right next door if you need anything," He added before stepping out to join Chelsea in the hallway. "That was nice of you."

"I told you this would be something Kelly would remember always. When is Santa going to get here?"

"They got hung up with the new snow coming down, but they'll be here in twenty minutes. It gives us just enough time to…" He nodded to the room he had taken over and opened the door.

"To what?" She followed him into the room, and noticed the table set up. Candles and dinner.

"I didn't have time for food and I thought you might join me. I'll apologize in advance because it's hospital food, but unless you wanted Chinese again it was the best I could do." He lit the candles and motioned for her to join him. "Chicken, baked potatoes, and broccoli. Nothing special."

"Every time I'm around you, you're trying to feed me."

"Food is the way to a woman's heart."

She laughed and sank down onto the chair. "That's supposed to be a man's heart. Women like to be romanced."

"Then I better step up my game because hospital food in a crummy crash room isn't going to cut it."

"I don't know about that." She smirked.

If she didn't know better she'd think he was actually trying to romance her, instead of just being nice to her. Or maybe it was wishful thinking, hoping he found her as desirable as she found him. She was a divorcee, with a deceased daughter, and no career besides her nonprofit organization. There was no chance Le was interested in her as anything but a friend.

"You okay? You seem distant."

She shook her head, clearing away the cobwebs. "I'm fine, just thinking."

"I'm sorry, is this too much for you? It's similar to—"

"No." She stopped him before he could finish. "Don't get me wrong. I miss Hope every day, but this has nothing to do with her. If anything, it's why I can relate to what Kelly's going through."

"I only meant you might not want to deal with this. We're coming up on the anniversary of Hope's passing."

"Don't you think I know that?" She snapped before pulling herself together. "Sorry. Damn it, I'm sorry. I'm just tired of everyone asking, walking around on eggshells. I've heard from Elizabeth five times in two days wanting to know how I was doing."

"Everyone's just worried about you, that's all." He reached across the table and placed his hand over hers, giving it a squeeze. "I'm here for you."

"Thank you." She forced the smile to return to her face. "Honest, I'm fine."

"Liz doesn't know when to step back. She's overbearing to anyone she cares about and I know you two have gotten close."

"Yeah." She smiled. Liz always meant well, but she wanted Liz as a friend not a counselor. She'd adjusted to her life, and though she would much prefer Hope had lived, she had found peace.

"You did the pajama exchange with Hope. I remember." He paused until she met his gaze. "I stopped by the hospital early on Christmas morning. You were asleep by Hope's bed, but she was awake, she was so happy about her cute new pajamas."

"They had little puppy dogs on it. That's all she wanted for Christmas, a puppy." Tears sprang to her eyes and this time she couldn't blink them away. "The one thing I couldn't give her."

"Oh, Chels." He went to her, wrapping his arms around her. "You'd have given her anything and she knew that. She knew a puppy wasn't something she could have in the hospital."

"I know." She wiped the tears away. "Sorry." She found herself apologizing again.

"There's no reason to be."

"It just hit me all over again." Wrapping her arm around him, she clung to him. "Kelly's going to be in the same position, and right now all that matters is giving her a few memories that don't completely involve being stuck in the hospital."

"That's what this is all about."

"Tomorrow is their Christmas and I want everything to be perfect." She let her head fall against his chest, breathing in his cologne, allowing it to relax her. "Let's eat. Santa will be here shortly and I have to tell him my Christmas wish."

It was time she began to live her life again. She wanted to love and be loved by someone. *Not someone, only Le.*

Circumstance had brought them together this Christmas because they both needed each other. It was possible to have everything they wanted in life. He could have his career, she could continue with Hope's Toy Chest, and there was plenty of time left over for love. No one would understand their needs and careers as the two of them did.

This Christmas was about love. For them *and* for the Cooks.

Chapter Eleven

Kingsley leaned against the wall, keeping out of the way as Santa reached down and scooped Jessica out of bed with great care, placing her delicately on his lap. Santa obviously had years of experience lifting sick children; he gave her the support she needed to stay upright, minding the IV lines.

"Thank you, Doctor Mathews, this is just what she needed. Look how happy she is," Kelly whispered to him before returning to her daughter's side.

"She's right. Look at Jessica glow with excitement." Chelsea stood next to him with her camera in hand, documenting every moment for Kelly.

He nodded, content things were going as planned. Assuming Jessica's fever didn't return, they could have their Christmas celebration. He'd spend the night right next door just in case anything went wrong. Not that he thought it would—as long as Kelly made sure Jessica didn't overdo herself.

"Merry Christmas, Jessica." Santa ran his hand over Jessica's back, soothing her as they waited for another coughing fit to pass. "What can Santa bring you for Christmas this year?"

Le sucked in a breath, waiting, praying her wish was something they could give her. If she asked for a cure it might break what little spirit he had, because that was one thing they didn't have, and wouldn't for quite some time.

"Come on, sweetie, tell Santa what you want," Kelly urged her daughter.

"My tiger."

"Honey, Santa wants to know what he can bring you. That tiger is at our house."

"Tell me about this tiger." Santa smiled down at her through his thick white beard.

"It's huge and soft. I want to cuddle with it." Jessica paused and a let out a deep yawn. "I feel safe with it. Please, Santa."

Santa glanced at Le before nodding. "I'll see what I can do, but is there anything else you'd like?"

"A new doll, one with pajamas like I'm always stuck in. Dresses make me miss going shopping with Mommy."

"Well, before Santa leaves, Mrs. Claus has something special for you." Santa cleared his throat and in stepped Grace dressed in a red velvet dress to match Santa's suit, even a black belt around her waist. Her hair was hidden under a wig, whitish gray to complete the outfit.

"Santa tells me you have a sweet tooth, so I brought your favorite chocolate cake." Carrying the cake, Mrs. Claus neared a wide-eyed Jessica.

"Chocolate cake." She glanced back to Le. "Can I, Doctor Mathews?"

"If you're going to share with the rest of us. After all, it's Christmas." He smiled at her as Chelsea handed Kelly plates and silverware.

"Let's eat." She smiled and forced herself farther up on Santa's lap. "Thank you, Santa and Mrs. Claus, this is the best Christmas ever."

Le couldn't help but think that if a miracle came to pass, it really would be the best Christmas. Otherwise it had a twinge of sadness hanging over it. How would Kelly handle things next year?

Santa sat Jessica back on the bed, carefully bracing her against the mountain of pillows so she could sit up and eat the cake. "Tomorrow when you wake up you'll have everything your heart could wish for."

"Thank you, Santa." Jessica's attention was now devoted to the cake.

"Santa, when do the rest of us get our Christmas wishes? I think Chelsea would like to tell you what she wants under her tree." Le caught her giving him a glare that warned him to tread carefully. "What? You said you had something you wanted to ask Santa for."

"I don't think this is the time. He needs to get back to the North Pole for Jessica's presents." Chelsea handed Le a piece of the cake before she took a seat on the spare unmade bed.

"I think I know her Christmas wish," Santa said. "But eat your cake and then you can tell me all about it on the way to my sled." Santa took the plate Mrs. Claus handed him.

"I'll be sure to do that." Chelsea took a bite of her cake. "Oh this is delicious."

"Can I have a ride in your sled?" Jessica's fork stopped in mid-motion to her mouth.

"Sorry, little one, but that's out of the question." Le answered before Santa or even Kelly could.

"Why not?" She laid her fork down and crossed her arms over her small body.

"Sweetie, you're not well enough to leave the hospital." Kelly sat on the edge of the bed. "Doctor Mathews was kind enough to arrange this celebration for us, so let's not push it. Okay?"

"Okay." Jessica reluctantly agreed. "Then can I have another piece of cake?"

"Doctor?" Kelly turned to him.

"One more." He nodded. "Then you should get some rest so Santa can bring your presents while you're sleeping."

"Yes, Doctor Mathews." Jessica tried to stifle a yawn as she took another bite.

Kelly stepped away from her daughter's bed and came across the room to him. "This is wonderful. Thank you."

"I couldn't have done it without Chelsea, Santa, and Mrs. Claus." Le took Kelly's hands, squeezing them gently between his own. "I'm glad we were able to do this for her."

"Me too. Very glad."

With the cake finished and Jessica dozing in the bed, Le completed one last check of his patient. While he double-checked her vitals and temperature, his gaze traveled to where Chelsea and Santa stood whispering on the other side of the room. What were they talking about? Whatever she had discussed with Santa, they had glanced his way and Chelsea was smirking knowingly. He heard her melodious giggle. Was she telling him her wish? He had hoped her Christmas wish would have been something he could have given her personally; instead, she was keeping it from him.

He'd like to be her Christmas wish, giving them both something to celebrate this year. Naughty images of being spread out under her tree in only a bow filled his thoughts. Damn, she stirred things deep within him he'd thought were long gone. He only hoped she was different. If they could be together, he hoped it would work. He hoped with every fiber of his being.

Hope's Toy Chest: Cedar Grove Medical

Chapter Twelve

With the Christmas celebration off without a hitch, Kingsley leaned back in his office chair, a mixture of happiness and exhaustion coursing through him. It was something that was sure to leave Kelly with the best memories when the worst happened. He was quite proud of himself and Chelsea for pulling it off.

His cell phone rang. With a silent prayer that it wasn't an emergency, he answered it. "Doctor Mathews."

"Le, it's Chelsea. I called Liz and got your number."

He sat up straight. "I was just thinking about you. Is everything okay?"

"Yeah. I was just wondering how the Cooks are doing. Have you moved Jessica back downstairs?"

"No, Nancy is staying upstairs with them for one final night. She'll be moved back down in the morning before her next treatment. I was just getting ready to leave. Are you at my house?" He hoped she was because he wanted to see her.

"Yeah. I thought I would cook us dinner if you were coming back soon. It will be a way to repay you for allowing me to take over your house, and all the meals you've fed me."

He glanced at the pile of paperwork and decided it could wait until the next day. "I'll be there in about thirty minutes. Shall I pick anything up on my way? A bottle of wine perhaps?"

"I already have one chilling. Just bring yourself and your appetite."

"I'll see you soon."

He could get used to the idea of someone waiting at home for him. In that moment he realized just what others saw in having a life outside the hospital. Maybe having Liz pressure him to find something or someone outside of his career wasn't such a bad thing. Love was something everyone should have. There were ways to balance his career and romance as long as it was with the right person. Chelsea was the right person for him, he knew that. In his heart, he knew they could make it work.

A whole chicken with oranges and vegetables roasted in the oven, a salad with a colorful arrangement of vegetables sat on the table, and homemade rolls were waiting to go into the oven. It was a simple dinner but one Chelsea was sure Le would enjoy. She suspected he didn't get many home cooked meals except when he went to Liz's. After everything he'd done, he deserved something special in return.

When she spoke to Liz earlier that day, she had been encouraging, as if she wanted them to end up together. Shaking her head, she put the final touches on the cheesecake. There wasn't a chance he'd ever see her as anything more than just a friend and she wasn't sure she was ready for any kind of relationship after her marriage had gone sour.

The front door opened and she heard Le call out. "I'm home."

Home.

What was it like to have a home? She couldn't remember any longer. She had an apartment, but living alone it wasn't a home. Her daughter had made it a home.

He strolled into the kitchen, his white dress shirt taut against his chest. "Something smells delicious."

"Roasted orange chicken." She leaned against the counter, the curve of the granite cool against her back. "It will be ready in thirty minutes."

"If you don't need me, I'd love to shower and change." He loosed the knot of his tie.

"Go ahead. The chicken needs twenty minutes and then I'll put the rolls in." With a quick nod, he disappeared down the hallway to the master bedroom, her gaze following the way the slacks cupped his butt.

"Get back to work." She whispered to herself before turning back to the strawberries that needed to be cut before dinner.

As she worked on the strawberries, her mind wandered as she imagined suds running down his body. Since Le had stepped back into her life, she couldn't keep him out of her fantasies. Knowing he was just down the hall and naked heated her body from the inside out.

She leaned against the corner of the counter, letting the sharp edge dig into her hands as she pictured him naked. Water cascading over his chest, little ripples falling down his body, along the sweet curve of his butt and down his legs. Her body heated with lust and need.

Her vibrating cell phone pulled her back a second before she made a fool of herself and went to him. She slipped it out of her pocket and tried to shake the thoughts free. "Hello." It came out a little too breathy and full of desire.

"Mrs. Waters?" A woman's voice spoke on the other end.

"Yes, this is she. Who's this?"

"My name is Jamie Hopkins. My daughter and I collected toys at my office and around town for your organization. Mrs. West, the grief counselor at Cedar Grove Children's Hospital is the one I've been going through, however I've been trying to get in touch with her for two days and she's been out of the office. Not knowing what else to do I found your number on the website for Hope's Toy Chest."

"Mrs. West should be back in the day after tomorrow, but is there something I can help you with?" Chelsea was disappointed and thankful for the interruption to her fantasies.

"I had expected to bring all these toys down to you, but I was in a nasty car accident and can't drive. I don't know what to do to get these to you, and I'd hate for all my daughter's hard work to be for nothing. Everyone I know who could make the trip is busy with the upcoming holidays, and Monday my daughter and I leave to meet her father in Germany for the holidays."

Monday. That meant she only had that weekend if she was going to get the toys.

"I'm sorry to hear about your accident. We can see about working something out. Where are you located?"

"It's a little over a two hour drive, I'm in Three Forks. I'm sorry, this was supposed to be something great and giving back to the hospital that helped save my daughter. Now I've just made a mess of it all." Tears coated the woman's words.

"No, it's wonderful that you did a collection. I appreciate it. Let me see what I can arrange for this weekend. Can I reach you at this number?" She wasn't sure how she'd do it, but somehow those toys would be picked up before the woman left for Germany. She knew the type of work and dedication it took and there was no way she'd let it be for nothing.

"Yes, I'm available at this number anytime. Thank you."

"You're welcome and I'll be in touch soon."

She ended the call and pulled up the weather app on her phone. Earlier that day there had been talk of a snowstorm heading toward them, so she needed to see how bad it was supposed to get. The mountains she'd have to pass over would make the trip terrible if there was a nasty storm. She'd have to look into renting a four-wheel drive vehicle, because her little car wouldn't make it this time of year.

"Anything I can do?"

She looked up to find Le standing beside the table in a pair of faded blue jeans and a gray T-shirt. Never before had she seen him in anything but dress clothes, and the casual fashion suited him. He looked amazing.

"Ahh...everything's almost ready. I just needed a minute."

"Everything okay?" He pulled out the chair next to her and sat down.

"I received a call about toy donations, but I need to go pick them up."

"Surely it can wait until after dinner, then I'll drive."

"I appreciate the offer but it's a little more complicated than that." She locked her phone and pushed it away from her. "The woman's daughter was brought to Cedar Grove, I'm not sure when or for what, but it must have been a good experience because they did a collection. The woman was in a car accident and can't make the trip to deliver the toys. They leave for Germany on Monday so I'll have to make arrangements to pick up the stuff this weekend."

"There's a snowstorm coming in. Where are they located?"

"Three Forks." She frowned, knowing it wasn't going to be an easy trip.

"Hmm, that could be a nasty journey and your car won't handle those mountains with snow very well."

"I'll call about renting something in the morning. They put in a lot of time and effort to do this, I can't let them down."

"Let me make arrangements to have someone cover me at the hospital if anything comes up, and we'll go Friday morning."

"You don't have to." She didn't miss the fact he was taking time off work to help her with this.

"I want to." He placed his hand over hers. "I'd like to accompany you on the trip if you'd have me. The weather's going to be bad and my truck can handle those roads better than your car. It also will allow you the whole truck bed for whatever she's collected."

"What about the hospital? The Cooks?"

"I can do my rounds early Friday morning, check on everything, and then we can leave. Another doctor can cover for me if anything comes up, and I can be reached on the phone if anything happens." His fingers teased along her knuckles. "If you don't want me to go, all you have to do is say so."

"No, I want you to go. It would be nice to have company, I just don't want to put you out." Suddenly she felt like she was on eggshells, like she had been when they first met. The unease tightened the muscles between her shoulders.

"Then it's settled. We'll leave early Friday morning and everything is going to work out just fine."

She smiled with both nervousness and excitement. The idea of being alone with him, driving through a snowstorm, seemed dangerous and appealing. To have him all to herself with no distractions was more than she could hope for.

Now if she could only find a way to get him naked.

Hope's Toy Chest: Cedar Grove Medical

Chapter Thirteen

The next day passed with incredible slowness. Le found himself looking at the clock thinking an hour or more had passed when in reality it had only been a few minutes. He was anxious for their trip, even if it would only allow them to spend a few additional hours together. He was supposed to be putting distance between them, keeping her out of reach before he couldn't keep his feelings to himself any longer. Instead he was offering to go on a road trip with her. How was he supposed to keep any distance between them while they were locked in his truck all day?

He leaned his head back against the leather chair and closed his eyes. Immediately his mind conjured an image of her in that body-hugging cami shirt she had on the night before, after she slipped out of her sweater when the heat of the fireplace and oven had overwhelmed her. Damn, he practically had to sit on his hands to keep them to himself. He hadn't had this much trouble controlling his desires since he was a teenager.

Someone stood in the door clearing their throat, pulling him from his thoughts before they could turn too erotic. He found his sister watching him with amusement.

"I'd ask you if you had a rough night, but I already know Chelsea was there until nearly one in the morning." She stepped into the office and closed the door.

"What's your point, little sister?"

"Just not used to you having a life outside of this place. Is there anything I should know?"

"Yes, there is." He leaned forward, placing his hands on the desk. "You should know to mind your own business. Do you see me butting into your life?"

"Actually, yes." She took the chair across from him. "You've always known everything that goes on in my life and you questioned Jason so thoroughly he thought he was on trial for murder."

"I'm the older brother; it's my job. Now was there something you wanted or did you just stop by to harass me?"

"Now that Jason's parents are here, we're having Brian over on Sunday, so I wanted to invite you and Chelsea as well."

Normally he'd agree without hesitation. Going over to Liz's meant a home cooked meal and good company. The fact she invited Chelsea made him question Liz's motives.

"I've seen that look before. I invited Chelsea because she's a friend of mine, and at this time of year no one deserves to be alone. She already agreed to come for Christmas dinner. So if there's unsettled waters between you two, you better deal with it quickly."

She stood but didn't move away from the desk. "She's a wonderful woman, and as you know she's been through a lot of shit. If you're not interested in something long term with her, don't lead her on. She deserves better than that. Now I'll see you Sunday at six. Have a safe trip."

Before he could argue that he couldn't get involved with Chelsea because she deserved so much more, Liz was gone. Just like Liz, leaving before he could defend himself. She had never been fond of confrontation.

Nevertheless, she was right; he couldn't lead Chelsea on. Either he had to be straight with her about his feelings, or he had to put distance between them. Neither one was going to be easy for him.

With nothing else to do but get back to the paperwork that littered his desk, he vowed to talk to Chelsea after their trip. She deserved him to be upfront with her. In the meantime, he had to decide if he was willing to give up what he could have with her before they even had a chance to explore it.

As he opened the next file on his desk that needed his attention, his cell went off with an emergency message.

Code blue: radiation room three. Glancing at the clock again, he jumped out of his chair and charged for the door. At that time of day, his only patient in radiation was Jessica. *Damn!*

Skipping the elevator, he raced down three flights of steps to the radiation ward. He wasn't a religious man, but with each step he said a silent prayer. Jessica's frail body couldn't take much more and if her heart stopped they might not be able to get it restarted. He made a mental note to talk to Mrs. Cook to see if she had changed her mind on a living willing for Jessica. Kelly needed to consider if she wanted them to perform extreme measures to try to save Jessica…or if she preferred them to let nature take its course.

He realized his thoughts sounded too similar to what the nurse had said, and he scolded himself. Coming through the stairwell doors, he didn't have time to consider it. Doctor Cole Roberts, the pediatric radiation oncologist handling Jessica's treatment, and one of his nurses stood waiting outside room three.

"What happened?"

Cole tipped his head to the side, dismissing the nurse before turning to Le. "We just finished Jessica's treatment when suddenly she said something was wrong. She didn't have time to explain before she went into cardiac arrest. After a flat line, we were able to get her heart beating again. Doctor West is with her now."

"Damn it." Le grabbed hold of the door handle. He was glad it was Brian in there with her. He was a good pediatric cardiologist and held the same beliefs as he when it came to saving children.

"Her heart and body are giving out, and you know the probability of her surviving this latest round of cancer. Is it wise to continue the treatments?"

"It's our duty to do everything we can to help our patients," Le reminded him, his tone heated with anger.

"We also made a vow not to do harm. Have you considered the treatment might be doing more harm than good?"

He had considered it but wasn't willing to admit it yet because that would mean defeat. The minute they stopped doing the treatments it would be an automatic death sentence for her.

"All I'm asking is for you to run a new batch of tests, see if we're making any progress with this treatment. If there are no changes, sit down with her mother and consider the options. Will you at least do that?"

Le nodded. "I won't put her heart under anymore strain until Brian clears her."

"Very well. With today's reaction, we'll postpone her treatment for tomorrow in order to give you time to perform the tests."

He opened to door, stepped inside, and found Kelly hovering by Jessica's bed. Tears streaked her face.

"I hear you had a negative reaction to the treatment. How are you feeling now?" Le asked.

"Tired." Jessica's voice was faint, and her eyes fluttered.

"Why don't you rest here for a few minutes while I speak with Doctor Mathews and your Mom?" Brian patted her hand. "Would that be okay? We'll just be right outside in the hall."

Jessica nodded, not opening her eyes, and Kelly kissed her forehead. "I'll be right back, sweetie."

Le opened the door for Kelly and Brian and when they stepped outside, he left it slightly opened so they could watch Jessica.

"How is she?" Kelly asked.

"Her heartbeat is faint and she's extremely tired. This episode took a lot out of her," Brian explained. "I need to do a chest x-ray,

EKG, and a few other tests before I can rule out any lasting damage."

"Is it from the treatment?"

"I can't say for sure. All I can say is she's a very sick little girl." Even as Brain spoke, there was something in his eyes that made Le wonder if he suspected the underlying cause but didn't want to worry her. "I'll get a nurse to take her for the tests and then she can go back to her room and rest. I'll check on her after I have the results."

"When she's brought back upstairs, I also want to do a full blood work up again," Le added. "It can wait until after your tests, or even tomorrow. We don't want to put her through any more than we have to today."

"I want her to take it easy for the rest of the day," Brian ordered. "Make sure she stays in bed, and no strenuous activities or we'll have to sedate her. I don't want any more damage until we know what caused this episode."

"She'll take it easy," Kelly promised and went back to Jessica's bedside.

Now that they were alone, Le nodded for Brian to follow him farther down the hall, giving them a little more privacy. "Do you believe the treatments caused this?"

"I believe this is one of the cases where there are no easy choices."

"Brian, we've known each another a long time. Just give it to me straight."

"It's a possibility. I'll know more when the tests are finished." He shoved his hands into the pockets of his white lab coat and nodded. "Okay. It's more likely that it's from the treatment than not."

It was what he'd expected, but it wasn't the news he wanted to hear. She would either die from her cancer if they stopped the treatments, or her heart would give out if they continued. Nothing was easy.

Hope's Toy Chest: Cedar Grove Medical

Chapter Fourteen

Silence cloaked the interior of the truck until it was uncomfortable. Le couldn't think of anything to say to make the trip easier, all he could think about was Jessica's pending test results. The early results from her EKG didn't hold much good news, but it was right after the incident, so they were rerunning it that afternoon. The other test results had left him scratching his head.

"Is everything all right?"

He nodded, not bothering to take his eyes off the road. The roads were quickly deteriorating and darkness was falling. They had been in Three Forks longer than he expected, putting them on the road late.

Silence threatened to overwhelm them again until he cleared his throat. "It's work. I'm sorry, I didn't mean for it to cause this unease."

"Anything I can do?"

"Unless you have a magical ability to make my cell phone ring, I don't think so." He tried to make light of it.

"I thought we didn't want your phone to ring. Wouldn't that mean there's an emergency at the hospital?" She turned slightly in the seat to look at him.

"We're running some tests on Jessica and I'm waiting on the results." He tugged the wheel to the right as it started to slide on some ice.

"Roads are getting bad."

"Yes, they are." He said between clenched teeth as he tried to keep the truck on the pavement. "With the way it's coming down and the drop in temperature I'm not sure we'll make it back tonight."

"What will we do?"

"There's a little hotel we passed on our way, it should only be a few miles up the road. I think we should stay there for the night and set out in the morning. It's only going to get worse." After regaining full control of the truck, he glanced over at her. "I'm sorry, but it would be for the best."

"That's fine, it's not worth risking our lives and maybe then you can call the hospital for an update."

He smiled, knowing that he wanted more than to just call the hospital. Eager to get off the road and alone with her, he continued to manhandle the truck forward.

Kingsley wasn't sure if he should be praising or cursing his luck. The small family-run hotel only had one room available with a single queen size bed. That was going to make things intimate and possibly awkward between them.

"Let me make a call and then we can go up to the dining room for a bite to eat. The owner's only serving for another hour and then we're out of luck, so I hope you're hungry." He slipped his cell phone out of the pocket of his jeans and was thankful when he saw he still had full service.

"I could go get the food and bring it back here. It will give you privacy for your call and we can have a quiet meal afterward." She grabbed her coat off the back of the chair and slipped it on.

"You don't have to do that."

"I'd rather have a quiet dinner here with you, if you don't mind." She pulled a crocheted blue and white hat over her blonde hair. "Make your call, I'll be back shortly."

He watched her slip out the door, the knowledge of what he wanted settling over him. Pushing his personal life to the side, he slid his thumb over the screen of his phone and called Brian.

"Kingsley, I was just about to call you. Are you coming back in this evening?" Brian asked.

"No, I'm not going to back in back into town until tomorrow. The weather got nasty and we've taken shelter. Is something wrong?"

"Not wrong." There was a shuffle of papers before Brian continued. "Different. I didn't call early because I wanted to double check the results."

"What are they showing?" He paced the small room unable to stay still.

"I'm not an oncologist but I believe your patient is in remission. All signs point to it."

"That can't be." He leaned against the wall, not sure he heard correctly.

"Do you have access to a computer and internet? I'll forward you the results, then you can see for yourself."

"Send them, I have my tablet." Leaving the hospital with his tablet in hand had been an accident and now it turned out to be a blessing. "I ordered another test when I was there this morning, but the results won't be back until tomorrow afternoon. In the meantime don't mention this to Mrs. Cook. I don't want to get her hopes up unless we are completely sure."

"She was praying for a miracle, and she might have gotten one."

"I hope so." He knew test results could be wrong but it was unlikely. "How about her heart?"

"She's weak, her body is tired, and it has taken its toll. With a little time, she'll be fine."

"Time…yesterday we didn't think she had any left." It all sounded too good to be true and until he saw the test results, he couldn't quite convince himself it was real.

"I'm sending them now. Give me a call if you have any questions, otherwise I'll see you when you get back."

After hanging up with Brian, Le slid down the wall to sit on the floor. Part of him wanted to rush out and get the tablet to check the results, while the other part of him screamed it might be a mistake. Jessica's chances at remission were less than one percent. The likelihood that she would live past the end of the year was barely ten percent. He couldn't help but think someone had messed up.

The door opened and Chelsea entered with a tray full of food. "Le?" She rushed to set the tray aside, then came to him. "What's wrong? Bad news?"

"Test results came back and I'm having a hard time believing them. I need to check them for myself. You go ahead and eat."

She shook her head. "I'll wait for you. How are you going to check them?"

"My tablet is in the truck." He wrapped his arm around her waist, pulling her onto his outstretched legs, and snuggling her against him.

"You're going to get yourself wet, I'm covered in snow."

"I don't care." He tugged her hat off. She was beautiful with her hair cascading down around her. Without thinking it through or giving himself a second to question himself, he leaned in and kissed her.

Claiming her lips with his own, he tasted the spiciness of cinnamon from the tea she had earlier, mixed with vanilla lip-gloss. He used his tongue to gently ease her mouth open. She leaned closer, her hand traveling up his chest as he kissed her one final time before pulling back.

"That was nice." Her breath was warm and full of desire.

"Nice? Hmm, I had hoped for better than nice."

"I meant…well, it was unexpected. You're out of my league." She started to pull away, but he held her tight.

"What is that supposed to mean?"

"It means just what I said. Look at us, you're the Chief of the Pediatric Oncology ward and I'm just a charity president, with no real career or life outside of it."

"You're so much more than that." He slipped a strand of her hair behind her ear. "Since you showed up in my life again, I can't get you out of my thoughts. You're all I think about lately. I'll admit I had planned to put distance between us, but not for the reasons you think."

"Then why?"

"You deserve so much better than what I can give you. Someone who will be home in the evenings, not off trying to save everyone that comes through the hospital doors." He locked his arms around her waist. "Chelsea, I work long hours, and even when I'm home I'm often working or thinking about work. What kind of life is that for you?"

"Many doctors find a way to balance a personal life and their careers. If anyone should understand what you do, I can. Those children and parents need you. You're an amazing doctor and I would never ask you to put your career on the back burner." She cupped the side of his face. "It seems as though we were both fighting this for our own reasons, and they aren't very different."

"What do you mean?"

"You've been haunting my fantasies and dreams since I showed up at your house and you knocked me on my ass. I was fighting it because I didn't want to come between you and the children you fight to save. I would never want to be the reason you missed something." She teased her finger along his jawline. "Now that we've gotten that out of the way. Why don't you kiss me again?"

Hope's Toy Chest: Cedar Grove Medical

Chapter Fifteen

With dinner finished and the test results still fresh in Le's mind, he sank down on the sofa next to Chelsea. Slipping his arm around her shoulders, he let his head fall back. The miracle the Cooks wanted had arrived, leaving him anxious to get back to Cedar Grove to deliver the news personally.

"You seem happier than I've ever seen you." She tipped her head until it was resting on his chest.

"For the first time in a very long time, I believe in miracles again."

"Sorry you're not there to…"

He lifted her chin with his forefinger. "Don't be sorry. I'm right where I want to be."

Without a second of hesitation, he leaned forward and their lips met with intense desire. Her mouth slid open, letting his tongue explore her. He slipped his hand along her body to her waist before pulling her into his lap. Sliding on top of him, she placed her knees on either side of him, all without breaking the kiss, her arms locked around his neck, drawing them closer.

Passion pulsated in his groin. He wanted nothing more than to take her to bed and have her scream his name. He broke the kiss, enjoying her warm breath over his face.

"Are you sure? You know what I can offer you…"

"Shhh." She placed her finger over his lips. "I'm sure. Are you?"

For a brief second, Liz's warning ran through his mind.

Don't lead her on…she deserves better than that.

He might not be the man he thought she deserved, but he'd do his best to make sure she never regretted this decision. "I've wanted you since you walked back into my life. I don't think I've ever wanted to be with someone as much as I want you." Adrenaline flooded his veins.

"Then let's not waste this night." She unlaced her hands from around his neck and pulled off her sweater, revealing a black bra with pink trim.

Without further invitation, he stood, taking her with him, and in two quick strides made it to the bed. He lowered her onto the mattress and whisked his shirt over his head.

"Take off your bra and lay back."

She did as he asked, quickly tossing the bra aside before reclining on her elbows. He wedged his body between her legs, leaning into her. Trailing kisses along her neck, hunger coursed through him. He wanted to take his time, to get acquainted with every inch of her body. He claimed her nipples with his mouth, sucking each one, and flicking his tongue over them.

"Le," she moaned, and tugged at the button of his jeans.

Reluctantly, he released her nipple, rising up above her so he could gaze into her green eyes while his hands caught hold of her jeans and slid them down her legs. "You're beautiful."

Her cheeks reddened, and her fingers paused mid-motion from sliding his zipper down. "If I'm naked then I want you to be as well. Off with these." She tugged at his jeans.

He slipped off the bed and quickly took off the remainder of his clothes. "I want you on top, to see your body riding mine. I want to see your beauty in the light from the fireplace." He slipped onto the bed next to her, pulling her with him until she straddled his torso, and caressed the curves of her body.

He slid his hand between their bodies, his fingers teasing her sweet spot before entering her core, tantalizing her with yearning. She arched her back, giving his fingers deeper access. As the light from the fire accentuated her body, she rode his fingers to near orgasm before he stopped. He wanted to feel her orgasm around his shaft and not a minute before.

"Le, please, I need you." Her voice was full of desire.

He moved his hands to her hips and lifted her. "Up." When she hovered above him, he adjusted so his shaft stood just below her entry. He guided her down onto him. Filling her inch by inch, nearly halfway in, he pushed up on her hips making her rise again before entering her completely with his manhood. His steady strokes fed her fire like tinder set to dynamite. His hands on her hips set their pace.

He leaned into her, locking his mouth on her nipple and sucked until she moaned in pleasure. She quickened the movement, driving the force of each pump. His thrusts became deeper and faster, a perfect rhythm.

Her body tightened around his shaft and her nails dug into his chest. "Oh, Le!" She cried out as his own orgasm followed.

Breathless, he brushed her hair from her face. He wanted to see her. Chelsea's eyes were glossy and dreamy—the aftermath of amazing sex. Glowing with beauty, she sent a fresh wave of desire through him.

She slid off him, lying next to him. Snuggling next to his body, she sighed. "I can't believe we're here together."

He pulled the blanket over them. His breath returned to normal as contentment filled him. He cradled her, caressing her spine with long, lazy strokes. "Me either."

The morning light was peeking through the curtains, reminding Le they should get on the road before the second wave of the storm hit. Throughout the night they had made love more than they had slept, making it too early for their tired bodies. He teased his fingers down Chelsea's arm, enjoying the feeling of her snug against his body.

"We should go." She tipped her head up to look at him. "I know you want to go to the hospital before it gets late."

"I'm sorry." This was the reason he had avoided relationships, he always felt guilty that he was so devoted to his career.

"Don't be." She ran her hand across his cheek. "I knew who you were before I agreed to this. I'll never have a problem with it, trust me."

He kissed her, tugging her bottom lip into his mouth and letting his teeth scrap lightly over it. "Thank you for understanding."

"Then let's get going."

He snuggled his face into her hair, enjoying one last quiet moment between them. "I guess we should."

"Since we have to drive almost past your house maybe you can drop me off there. My car is still there." She slipped out of his embrace, edging toward the end of the bed.

"I was kind of hoping you'd come with me. Liz is off and Kelly might need someone to talk to in order to adjust to the newest development. With Liz's in-laws in town, I don't want to call her in if I don't have to."

"I don't think she'll want me or anyone else. I respect you can't tell me but I can make a logical jump, and she's only going to want to be with her daughter."

"We'll see. So will you come with me to the hospital, then we can go back to my place and deal with my exploding truck bed of toys?"

With a nod, she slipped on her jeans. "I'll stay in the waiting room, and you can let her know I'm there if she wants to talk. Now get dressed."

"Oh, I like a woman who thinks she's in charge." He wiggled his eyebrows at her. More like he enjoyed her feistiness. Submissive woman, always waiting for a man's orders, had never been his thing. He wanted a woman with her own mind, one who would stand beside him, not behind him.

"I can be in charge when needed, but this time I have my own motives."

"What's that?" He slipped out of bed and followed suit by pulling on his pants.

"I'm hoping once we leave the hospital I can have you to myself for a bit, and I wasn't thinking about the gifts in your truck."

That very thought sped him up. He wanted to be alone with her. If he'd had his way, they would've spent the rest of the weekend here, locked in each other's arms.

Chapter Sixteen

Kingsley sat behind his desk waiting for Kelly to say something, anything. Instead she just sat there silently, tears streaming down her face. Damn it, he should have called Liz in, he needed the backup when it came to crying women.

"Are you absolutely sure? How?"

"We ran the tests multiple times. Jessica is in remission." Even as he said it, he couldn't believe it. Since Jessica had come under his care there had never been a true remission. They had made progress with treatments for different periods but it always came back with a vengeance. "As for how, I'd love to take credit for it. To tell you it was the treatment, or modern medicine, but I can't."

"What?"

"As you know, we ran routine tests recently, and there was no change." He opened the file on his desk, needing to see the proof again. "These tests look as though she's been in remission for weeks. It's impossible."

"A miracle." She mumbled.

"The miracle you wanted." He leaned forward, placing his hands on the folder.

"Can I take her home?"

"I'm afraid we're not at that stage just yet." It was unbelievable that they were talking about Jessica leaving the hospital, when only a few days before they believed she wouldn't see Christmas. "She's weak and all of this has taken a toll on her body, especially her heart. Doctor West, the pediatric cardiologist you met the other day, has agreed to take Jessica as a patient. He'll be working to regain her health. When the time comes that she can leave the hospital, we want her in the best condition she can be in. Give it time."

"I'll give it all the time in the world because my little girl has been given a second chance at life. She's going to live." Tears followed freely down her face, but these were tears of joy. "Thank you."

He nodded, not sure what else to say. "Liz had plans today or she'd be here, but I know you connected with Chelsea. We just returned from Three Forks with a load of toys that were collected there by a former hospital patient and her mother. I got the news and came straight here. If you need someone to talk to, I'm sure she'd be willing, or I can call Liz."

"No, let Liz enjoy her day off. This isn't a time for a grief counselor. It's a time for celebration. Does Chelsea know?"

He shook his head. "You know I couldn't tell her. I only made her come with me so I didn't have to make a detour."

"Where is she? I'd like to tell her the news before I go to Jessica."

"The family lobby, just down the hall."

"Thank you for everything." She rose from the chair and reached to him, laying her hand over his.

"It was a miracle. One that was deserved." He didn't feel there was any credit due to him for this. It wasn't something he did, but it was something he sure wished he could replicate. "Now go to Chelsea so you can get back to Jessica. Just remember, she still needs to take it easy."

"You have my word." With that she slipped from his office.

Wanting to give Kelly and Chelsea time together, he looked over the file again hoping to find something that would explain it. Something that let him know how it happened. Maybe then he could do it again. He knew there should be a logical explanation somewhere, and perhaps it would point to the cure he was searching for.

Chelsea leaned against the doorframe watching Le scan the file in front of him. Knowing him as she did, she was sure he was looking for something logical to explain a miracle. From what she gathered, he wouldn't find anything.

She had a moment of sadness, wondering why Hope couldn't have had the same miracle. Then she realized that if the miracle had come then, she wouldn't be where she was now, and Hope's Toy Chest would have never been created. Without it, she wouldn't have been able to bring joy to children and parents each year. Maybe everything had happened for a reason.

She tapped her knuckle against the door, gaining his attention. "You're not going to find what you're looking for there. Some things are unexplainable. Look at Liz, she's here because of a miracle too." She wandered into the office and sank down into the chair across from him.

"You know I spent years trying to explain what happened with Liz."

She could picture him going through every page of Liz's file over and over again. Never solving the mystery he was so desperate to unravel. "I've always believed some things are best left undiscovered."

"Are you saying I shouldn't seek a cure for childhood cancers?" He leaned back, his eyes wide with shock.

"No, not at all." She shook her head, trying to find the best way to explain it. "What I'm saying is miracles happen, and if we go searching for the reason we'll drive ourselves crazy. Some believe that if you search too hard the miracle will cease and you'll be back where you started. I wouldn't want to test it."

"You sound a little too much like Liz." He twirled the pen between his fingers. "When she found out I got access to the files from her treatments…let's just say I think that was our very first fight."

"Why was she so upset?"

"She put it behind her, and doesn't want to relive it. I was never fully able to put it behind me. I see her in every child I treat, it's what drives me to find a cure. I thought I might be able to learn something by going over her records."

"Did you?"

He shook his head. "There was nothing I didn't know already from medical school and my years of training. I thought maybe because I was young I didn't know everything about her condition. That maybe somewhere in the file there'd be something. I even looked up the doctor who was in charge of her care."

"Sometimes the things that happen in life are unexplainable." She gave him a shy smile. "My mother always said you should never look a gift horse in the mouth, you might not like what you find."

"If I'm to find a cure then I need to tear this case apart over and over again until I find why she's suddenly in remission."

"What if you don't find what you're looking for? What if there are no answers in that file?"

"I'll go on to the next one, and the one after that. There's got to be something everyone is missing." He'd search his whole life if he had to, and that was pure dedication.

"If everyone else is missing it, why do you think you'll find it?" She admired him for his commitment, but she had to insert a touch of reality.

"Because I have to."

"Trust me, I want there to be a cure. I don't want to see these children suffer." She wiped her hands, stopping herself from going to him. "People have searched for a cure for years, it might not be something that's developed in our lifetimes. Right now, all you can do is treat it, learn from what worked in the past, but be flexible because it won't always work again. I have no medical experience besides what I went through with Hope, but I know each case is different and needs to be treated as such. You need to be grateful that Jessica's in remission and focus on your other patients."

"Don't you wonder why Jessica was saved when Hope's cancer was less invasive?"

Tears stung her eyes but she blinked them away. "No. It won't bring Hope back, and what matters is Jessica has a chance to live. If she's lucky she'll never have another battle with cancer and can go on to live a happy and healthy life. The Cooks have a blessing. I'm happy for them."

"Even though I wasn't able to give one to Hope?"

She had worried he felt guilty since he had been Hope's primary doctor, but none of it was his fault. She hoped whatever was happening between them wouldn't be spoiled by unreasonable guilt. "You did everything you could for her."

"If I had a cure I could have saved her."

"No, you might have been able to but there's no guarantee." She leaned forward, placing her hands on the desk. "What's happening between us could be a wonderful thing, but if you have some unshed guilt over what happened in Hope's treatment then we might never get this to go anywhere. I need you to be straight with me."

"Come here." He held his hand out to her, waiting until she came around the desk and then he pulled her onto his lap. "Logically I know I did everything I could to save your daughter. I used every option that was available to me. Nothing worked. I don't feel I was neglectful in her treatment or her care. I only have guilt because I want to save everyone."

"That's what will cause burnout." She cupped his cheek, forcing him to look up at her. "Then what good will you be to all the sick children in need of you?"

When he didn't answer she ran her thumb over his cheekbone. "You're an amazing man. Your love for children brought you to this profession for a reason. Maybe it isn't to find a cure for everyone, but to help those you can. You have to remember you can't save everyone, but you touch everyone's life. Even after Hope passed away and I was left to cope on my own I never forgot you…or what you did for us."

"I did nothing special."

"You did more than any other doctor would." She laced the fingers of her free hand through his. "That Christmas morning when Hope passed away you sat there comforting me. We went, grabbed coffee, and you held me as I cried. No other doctor would have done that. You missed your family celebration to be with me in my time of need and for that I'll always be grateful. Just as I know that Kelly and Jessica will never forget you or what you've done."

She realized this wasn't just about them, it was about everything. Cancer, a cure, the families he worked with. Suddenly she wondered if there wasn't more she could be doing to make the lives of these children better. Ideas raced around her mind; the biggest involved helping out at the hospital.

With Liz and Kingsley's aid, Hope's Toy Chest would be advancing to another level in the New Year. Her personal life was also quickly improving—because she'd be damned if she'd ever let him slip through her fingers.

Gently wrapping her arms around him, she pulled him close until her chest was pressed against his and their lips met. As the passion sparked between them, she knew she'd found something special. She'd been through so much, and she'd finally gotten what she needed most.

Chapter Seventeen

The next few weeks passed in a blur and Christmas Eve was upon them. When Le wasn't at the hospital, he was with Chelsea. It was the first time be actually had something outside of the hospital that he looked forward to, that he enjoyed. It didn't matter what they were doing—watching a movie, wrapping gifts, sharing a quiet meal—every moment he spent with her was perfect.

"Are you coming?" Chelsea hollered from the living room where she waited.

He took one last look in the mirror to make sure his beard was on perfectly. He couldn't be Santa with a crooked beard, and everyone was expecting him. With everything in place, he couldn't help but laugh at how ridiculous he looked. There he stood in his velvet red suit with white trim on the wrists and ankles, the wide black belt holding up the pillow hidden under his jacket, and the itchy beard.

"Oh, Santa…" A teasing voice called down the hall.

"Yes, Mrs. Claus, I'm coming." He spun on the heels of his black boots and found her standing in the doorway. Damn, she looked hot in the cute red dress, with a white sash tied around her waist.

"There's some special children waiting for Santa's visit."

"I know, and we have to deliver presents once they are asleep. I never realized how much work you do. Good thing we can sleep in tomorrow."

"Not too late. I promised Liz I'd help her with Christmas dinner."

"Dinner isn't until three, how early do we have to be there?"

"I told her I would be there at noon. There's plenty of time for us to have a luxury lay in." She sashayed toward him, swaying her hips in a way that instantly hardened his shaft.

He reached out, slinging his arm around her and pulled her close. "I don't think it would be good for Santa to have a hard-on when he's about to have dozens of kids on his lap."

"Maybe we should take care of it then." She slid her hand down his chest, easing toward his shaft.

"I'd love to take you up on that, but Liz and Jason are waiting for us. We can't be late." He pressed his lips to hers, letting her know just how desirable he found her. "Though I will tell you this, you'll be wearing this outfit for me again. I love the way it clings to your curves. You're one sexy Mrs. Claus."

"I'll have to see about keeping it out of storage for your pleasures." She smiled. "Now come along before I push you down on that bed and have my way with you."

He slipped his hand in hers and led the way to the door. Making his way through the house, he caught a glimpse of the nine foot Christmas tree they bought and decorated the week before. There it stood next to the fireplace, with its glowing white lights and ornaments the children made for him. Over the years, his collection had grown and now took up nearly the whole tree.

The spirit of Christmas had returned to him and was stronger than ever. Now he had to pass that same cheer on to others. Who could have guessed Hope's Toy Chest had something special for him too?

The sun was peeking around the edges of the curtains when Le opened his eyes, his arm around Chelsea keeping her snuggled against his body. It was the perfect start to a Christmas morning. The first Christmas of many more, or so he hoped.

"Morning." Chelsea's voice was groggy as she slid her leg over his. "What time is it?"

He glanced at the bedside clock. "A little after seven."

"Are you crazy?" Her eyes widened. "We didn't even get to bed until after three this morning. That's four hours of sleep, there's no way we're getting up yet. You promised a luxury lay in, remember?"

"That I did, but I never said we would be sleeping." He rolled her over, quickly positioning himself on top of her. "This is the latest I've slept in years. I think you own me for it."

"I owe you?" Now fully awake she raised her eyebrow in question.

"Yes and I intend to make sure you pay." He slid his hands under the red silk nightshirt she was wearing. Sliding his fingers along the curve of her hips, up her body, he took the nightshirt with him. "Lean up or I'll tear it off you."

"You can't do that, this was a gift from my very own Santa." She slid the nightshirt over her head, and his shaft hardened against her at the sight of her naked body.

"You never did tell Santa what you wanted this Christmas."

"I told Grace's husband, and it seems he delivered." She wrapped her arms around his neck, bringing him closer. "I wanted this...you."

"That's one wish I can grant." He slipped off her and quickly pulled off his shorts. "If I had known it was me you wanted, I would have wrapped myself up."

She let out a lighthearted chuckle. "Oh, would you have?"

"Well, maybe just a large bow."

"I'd like to see that." She pulled him closer to her. "Show me why it was worth getting up this early."

He grinned and slipped into the bed beside her, pressing his lips to hers. He stroked the length of her body and slid a hand between her legs in search of her core. His fingers delved inside, sending a quiver through her body. She rocked against him, arching into him and sending his fingers deeper within her.

Pressing his lips to hers, he worked his free hand through her hair, holding her tight to him. Feeling her moans against him. His lips tore from hers, working their way down her neck. "Not yet." He whispered, slipping his hand from between her legs and moving to hover over her. He nudged her legs farther apart with his knee.

She wrapped her legs around him, dragging him closer. "I need you." The desire laced her words.

"Unwrap your legs." He winked, giving her neck one final kiss.

"Le." She cried out when he hovered above her, watching her.

Without further demand, his mouth found her nipple as he slid his shaft into her, easing in until he was completely buried within her. She arched her body, her core muscles tightening around him, and her nails clawed into his back until he was sure she drew blood. He started slow—a pleasurable torture, an inexorable build. His hands roamed over her, petting her, teasing her. He loved how her body reacted to each touch.

"Faster." She clenched her inner muscles around his shaft, his thrusts growing deeper and faster, sending the world into a shimmering bliss. They rocked back and forth in rhythm, until she screamed for release. Calling his name as her body clenched around him and her fingers rubbed his back. His own ecstasy found him as he buried his shaft as deep within her as possible.

"Merry Christmas." He nuzzled against her neck, kissing the vulnerable point behind her ear. Sliding out of her, and off to the side, he knew he was in love with her.

"Merry Christmas." She snuggled against him, her fingers running over his chest.

It was time he grabbed life by the horns. "Chelsea." He leaned up on his elbow and looked down at her. "I've always lived my life around my hospital and patients. It wasn't until you came back into my life that I realized how important a life outside of the hospital was. What I'm trying to say is that I'm in love with you. Will you marry me?"

She ran her the back of her hand along the side of his face, teasing along his jaw line. "Yes." With a bright smile, she nodded. "I never thought I'd fall in love again, but I did. I love you, Kingsley."

He pulled her tight against him and kissed her. This was the best Christmas present he could have hoped for. "I'll get you a ring first thing tomorrow when the stores open."

"That doesn't matter. What matters is I have you."

"I'll do my best to make sure you never regret this. You'll be the happiest woman alive."

He knew he would keep his promise no matter the cost. Sometimes love meant sacrificing for those you cared for, and he'd give anything to keep her happy and by his side forever.

Chapter Eighteen

Chelsea thought she'd gone all out on decorations at Le's house but it was nothing compared to what Liz and Jason's place looked like. The inside of the two story brick home could have been Santa's workshop. A large tree dominated the foyer with a more moderately sized one in the living room. Garlands and lights were strung around the banister leading upstairs, an entire Christmas village lined the living room bookshelves, and not one but two old fashioned trains circled the base of the tree, letting off a blare of horns every time they passed the main section.

Appetizers, each one looking more delicious than the last, were spread out across the kitchen bar that separated it from the living room. People gathered around the table, or in the living room talking. Le took her around introducing her to his parents, then to Jason and Brian's parents. Years ago when Hope had been in the hospital, she'd met Brian, but they reacquainted themselves before Liz dashed in.

"Chelsea, come with me, I want to show you the rest of the house." She nodded toward the door and Chelsea followed.

She waited until they climbed the stairs before she laid a hand on Liz's arm. "I've been here before, so why did you want to get me away from everyone?"

"To show you this." Liz pushed open the door and she stepped closer to see what was inside.

A nursery, done in a pale pink, with white and black accents, the name *Faith* in fancy letters above an ebony crib. There was a changing table, dresser, and rocker that matched. The crib bedding was black with large white swirls and pink roses; the edges had vibrant pink trim.

"Are you? But I thought—"

"With the cancer treatments I went through as I child, I can't get pregnant, but we're adopting. Our beautiful baby girl is due on Valentine's Day."

"Le didn't say anything." She turned her head to look at her friend. "He doesn't know. Your brother doesn't know." Shock coated her words.

"No one but Jason knows. We didn't want to say anything until we were sure. The birth mother is a nurse's assistant at the hospital. She's young, single, and wants to go back to school for her registered nurse's license. It's going to be an open adoption, and Faith will know birth mother." Liz paused and looked back at the nursery. "It's everything I wanted and finally it's happening. I never thought I'd be a mother, but Susan is great. She's allowing me to come to her doctor's appointments, and I was there when we heard the heartbeat. Oh, Chelsea, it's more than I could have hoped for."

"When are you telling your family?"

"When we sit down for dinner. We've been holding off until everyone was gathered together. Susan will stop by later on so everyone can meet her and see our baby." Liz laid her hand on Chelsea's arm. "I wanted you to know first, because I know what a hard time of year this is for you. I didn't want to upset you."

"Oh no, Liz, don't worry about me. I'm happy for you." Memories of expecting Hope resurfaced. She'd never replace Hope in her heart or thoughts but she wondered if Le was interested in having children. They had never talked about it but she hoped he would be willing. She wanted to try again. It was time.

"Are you sure?"

"I am." Chelsea turned to her. "Actually, I was hoping to get a minute alone with you today because I have some news of my own."

"Spill it." Liz leaned back against the door frame and eyed her.

"Le asked me to marry him and I said yes."

"Oh, that's wonderful." Liz pulled Chelsea into a tight hug. "I'm so happy for the two of you. You do understand what you're getting into with his career, don't you?"

"Yes. First you're happy for me, then you follow it with a downer." She teased. "There was something else. Remember how you wanted me to talk with some of the parents who were having a hard time dealing with their child's cancer?"

"Yes, and you turned me down, saying you weren't ready for that."

"I am now if you need someone. I spoke with Kelly Cook, Jessica's mother, and I think I can do some good. I can meet with parents who are having a hard time, have coffee with them while they're waiting for the chemo or radiation treatments to be finished. I don't want the responsibility of your job, I just want to be a friend, someone to listen to them."

"We'll get you started right away. What changed your mind?"

"A little bit of this and that, but mostly talking to Kelly and Le. It's time I move on with my life. Hope will always be a part of me but I have to start living again. I've also got to show that brother of yours that there's more to life than just the hospital." She paused as she heard voices coming from below. As they passed, she turned back to Liz. "I also want to do more with Hope's Toy Chest but we can discuss that later. I believe you have some news you need to tell the family." She winked.

"Correction, news we *both* need to tell everyone. You're announcing your engagement too." Liz slipped her arm through Chelsea's and headed to the stairs.

"Oh no. This is your moment, they can find out about the impending wedding soon enough. I only told you because I couldn't hold it in any longer and I was hoping you'd be my maid of honor."

"Seriously?"

Chelsea nodded. "You're my best friend and his sister, there's no one else more qualified."

"Oh, this is going to be so much fun." Liz let go of her arm and bounced down the steps. "Everyone gather around! There are a few announcements we need to get out of the way before dinner. Le and Chelsea, why don't you do the honor."

"What are you talking about?" Le raised an eyebrow, glancing between both women.

"Sorry, I couldn't help myself." She smiled and held out her hand to him. "Tell everyone so Liz can tell them her good news." When he came to her, she wrapped her arm around his waist.

With his arm around her, she snuggled against him, glowing with happiness. Things had a way of working out and eventually she'd found contentment. No, on the contrary; it had found them.

Hope's Toy Chest: Cedar Grove Medical

Epilogue

A barbeque had sounded like a wonderful idea when Kingsley thought of it, but now that the day had arrived all he wanted to do was take his wife up to their room and forget about the last twenty-four hours. Ups and downs were part of a doctor's life, but when one of the patients he'd been seeing for years came out of remission, only to decline quickly, he began to wonder if things were worth it. With the grill going, he stared out at the green grass, his thoughts transporting him back to the hospital until he heard a familiar little girl's yell.

"Doctor Mathews!"

He looked to the side of the house to see Jessica sprinting toward him, her mother Kelly only a few steps behind. Six months of remission and she looked like any other child her age. A little skinnier than she should be, but she was up running around and not stuck in some hospital bed. "Jessica, it's good to see you, my Christmas miracle." He squatted down to give her a hug.

"It was nice of you to invite us." Kelly held a large bowl filled with fruit salad. "I know you said not to bring anything but I couldn't come empty-handed."

"Thank you, but we're just glad you could make it." Chelsea took the bowl and set it on the table.

"I hear you're doing amazing work at the hospital." Kelly squeezed Chelsea's arm. "Parents going through cancer with their children need someone like you to talk to." She leaned in to whisper, "But don't forget about your own life."

"Don't worry. For the first time I feel like I'm actually living. Things couldn't be better."

"We make time outside of our hospital duties." Le smirked, having overheard them. "Well, that and Hope's Toy Chest. If I don't stop her she's going to have the organization spread across the world."

"No, for right now I think I'll keep it home-based. I want my work to be enjoyed by the patients at Cedar Grove Children's Hospital." She slipped her arm around Le's waist.

"Chelsea is actually putting together a party for the children who are in remission. We had hoped Jessica would be one of our honored guests. She's truly a miracle and we want to celebrate that." Le looked down at Chelsea and smiled. She never ceased to amaze him.

"We'd be honored. It would be nice for her to meet other children her own age who have suffered what she has. She's so small for her age that some of the other children at the park make fun of her." Kelly frowned as she looked to Jessica. "My baby has been given a second chance but now she has another battle ahead of her—other kids. I couldn't protect her from cancer, and there's little I can do about the other children."

"Now that she's healthy, she'll begin to catch up to her peers. It will take time and she might always be smaller than her classmates but you'll begin to see the change in her." He glanced to Jessica, who was rolling around in the yard like a gymnast. "Sorry, but I still can't believe her recovery."

"Me neither. I keep waking up thinking it was a dream, but when I go down the hall to her bedroom and see her laying there it all comes back to me." Tears glistened in Kelly's eyes.

"That gives me another idea." Chelsea sat her glass of lemonade aside. "Why not start a regular playgroup for the children who are in remission or are well enough to attend? Then children can meet others their own age who understand what they've gone through and why they look different. There'd be no reason to try to hide and the ridicule would be minimal."

"Where would you hold it?" Le asked.

"I have a friend who owns a daycare facility, Cradles to Crayons. Last year she added a large indoor play area, with climbing structures, slides, and a large ball pit. It would be the perfect place to have it. We'd have it professionally cleaned before each play session to limit the chance of any of the children becoming sick. Maybe do it once a month."

"Oh, that would be nice and I know Jessica would just love it," Kelly exclaimed. "If you need any help I'd be glad to do whatever I can. Something like that would be good not only for the children but for the parents."

"I'll get started on it this week and let you know what I can use help with," Chelsea said as Kelly's cell phone chirped to life.

"Sorry, I have to take this." Kelly stepped away and brought the phone to her ear.

Le kissed the top of his wife's head. "You never cease to amaze me."

"Good. I like keeping you on your toes." She heard car doors shut around the front of the house announcing Liz's arrival. She wrapped her arms around him because once Liz arrived with Faith, he would be too preoccupied cuddling that little girl. "Before they get back here there's something I want to talk to you about."

"What is it?" He rubbed small circles along her hip.

"Do you want children?"

Children? His mind raced on how to answer it. Yes, he wanted children, but he knew when he married her it might not be an option. She might not want to have another child after what happened with Hope. As much as he would have liked children of his own, it wasn't as important as having Chelsea as his wife. He loved her and wanted to spend the rest of his life with her, with or without children.

He must have taken longer than she thought he needed to answer because she broke the silence.

"I want to have another child," she blurted out.

"Really?" He couldn't keep the surprise out of his voice.

She nodded. "I love Hope and that won't change no matter how many children I have. But she's not here any longer and it's time for me to move on. We both love children and can offer them the love and home they deserve. I want to have a baby with you."

"Then we'll do it because I've always wanted children too. But I didn't think you wanted another one." He pulled her around to face him. "I love you, Chelsea Mathews."

"As I love you, Kingsley."

He lowered his head to hers until he could claim her lips.

Hope's Toy Chest: Cedar Grove Medical

Marissa Dobson

Born and raised in the Pittsburgh, Pennsylvania area, Marissa Dobson now resides about an hour from Washington, D.C. She's a lady who likes to keep busy, and is always busy doing something. With two different college degrees, she believes you're never done learning.

Being the first daughter to an avid reader, this gave her the advantage of learning to read at a young age. Since learning to read she has always had her nose in a book. It wasn't until she was a teenager that she started writing down the stories she came up with.

Marissa is blessed with a wonderful supportive husband, Thomas. He's her other half and allows her to stay home and pursue her writing. He puts up with all her quirks and listens to her brainstorm in the middle of the night.

Her writing buddies Max (a cocker spaniel) and Dawne (a beagle mix) are always around to listen to her bounce ideas off them. They might not be able to answer, but they are helpful in their own ways.

She love to hear from readers so send her an email at marissa@marissadobson.com or visit her online at http://www.marissadobson.com.

Hope's Toy Chest: Cedar Grove Medical

Other Books by Marissa Dobson

Alaskan Tigers:

Tiger Time

The Tiger's Heart

Tigress for Two

Night with a Tiger

Trusting a Tiger

Jinx's Mate

Two for Protection

Bearing Secrets

Stormkin:

Storm Queen

Reaper:

A Touch of Death

Beyond Monogamy:

Theirs to Tresure

SEALed for You:

Ace in the Hole

Explosive Passion

Capturing a Diamond

Operation Family

Cedar Grove Medical:

Hope's Toy Chest

Destiny's Wish

Fate Series:

Snowy Fate

Sarah's Fate

Mason's Fate

As Fate Would Have It

Half Moon Harbor Resort:

Learning to Live

Learning What Love Is

Her Cowboy's Heart

Half Moon Harbor Resort Volume One

Clearwater:

Winterbloom

Unexpected Forever

Hope's Toy Chest: Cedar Grove Medical

Losing to Win

Christmas Countdown

The Surrogate

Clearwater Romance Volume One

Small Town Doctor

Stand Alone:

Secret Valentine

Restoring Love

The Twelve Seductive Days of Christmas

CPSIA information can be obtained at www.ICGtesting.com
Printed in the USA
LVOW07s1630100515

437948LV00001B/160/P

9 781939 978486